MURDER ON THE
SEA OTTER
EXPRESS

A GRACE "THE HIT MOM"
MYSTERY

ALSO BY NIKKI KNIGHT

PRAISE FOR THE
GRACE "THE HIT MOM" MYSTERIES

PRAISE FOR *MURDER ON THE SEA OTTER EXPRESS*

"Fast, funny, and wildly suspenseful, *Murder on the Sea Otter Express* takes the usual cozy mystery tropes and supercharges them. Author Nikki Knight begins with the familiar 'second shift' of working moms and gives it a whole new meaning, an inevitable result when the mom in question moonlights as a contract killer for a secret society of 'lady assassins.' Think of it as Miss Marple meets Batman. Or Jessica Fletcher meets Robin Hood. Either way, the whip-smart dialogue, engaging characters, and twisty plot will keep you reading from the first chapter to the deeply satisfying conclusion."

—**Lori Robbins**, Amazon bestselling author of the On Pointe and Master Class mystery series

"Grace Adair and the gang are back for more sleuthing, and this time the Hit-Mom is chaperoning a class trip to the aquarium. What could go wrong? Plenty, and Grace is embroiled in a twisted mystery full of revenge and dirty secrets. This is a page-turner of a mystery that will keep you on the edge of your seat."

—**Heather Weidner**, author of the Pearly Girls Mysteries and the Jules Keene Glamping Mysteries

PRAISE FOR *HOUND OF THE BONNEVILLES*

"[Nikki Knight] is really one of the best cozy writers at work at the moment."

—**Robin Agnew**, *Aunt Agatha's*

"*Hound of the Bonnevilles* checks every box for cozy mystery fans, and it does so in ways that will appeal to readers beyond that genre. With wit, and charm, and a twisty plot that delivers a most satisfying ending, it's a 2025 must-read."

—**Lori Robbins**, award-winning author of the On Pointe and Master Class mystery series

"Grace the 'Hit Mom' is back for more adventures in this fast-paced holiday mystery where no Grinch blowup is safe."

—**Heather Weidner**, author of the Pearly Girls Mysteries

PRAISE FOR *WRONG POISON*

"There's a certain feel to a book that's just right. Everything hits the mark just as it should. For me as a reviewer, that earns my highest praise, as a book that's 'just right' is as good as it can be, and in the case of Nikki Knight's *Wrong Poison*, that's very good indeed."

—*Aunt Agatha's*

"Smart, fast-paced dialogue, and characters to care about. Can't wait for the next one."

—**Eileen Curley Hammond**, author of *The Merry March Mysteries*

"Not your average cozy! A highly enjoyable modern mystery with a host of very real and memorable characters, a highly unusual heroine and lots of wit."

—**Geraldine Byrne**, author of the Caroline Jordan Mysteries

MURDER ON THE SEA OTTER EXPRESS

A GRACE "THE HIT MOM" MYSTERY

NIKKI KNIGHT

+ KEYLIGHT
BOOKS
AN IMPRINT
OF TURNER
PUBLISHING

Keylight Books
an imprint of Turner Publishing Company
Nashville, Tennessee
www.turnerpublishing.com

Murder on the Sea Otter Express

Cover design by J. Kent Holloway
Cat illustrated by Brianna Youngman
Book design by William Ruoto

Library of Congress Cataloging-in-Publication Data
Names: Knight, Nikki author
Title: Murder on the Sea Otter Express / by Nikki Knight.
Description: Nashville, Tennessee : Turner Publishing Company, 2026. I
Series: Hit Mom mysteries
Identifiers: LCCN 2025019656 (print) I LCCN 2025019657 (ebook) I
ISBN 9798887981222 paperback I ISBN 9798887981239 hardcover I ISBN
9798887981246 epub
Subjects: LCGFT: Cozy mysteries I Novels I Fiction
Classification: LCC PS3611.A4317 M87 2026 (print) I LCC PS3611.A4317
(ebook)
LC record available at https://lccn.loc.gov/2025019656
LC ebook record available at https://lccn.loc.gov/2025019657

Printed in the United States of America

For my son, Martin Kalb.
A mensch before he was a man.
The best of both his parents, but absolutely himself.
Impossible to love you more.

CHAPTER ONE
GREAT WHITE WHALE

W hen we went on the aquarium field trip, I never thought
anyone would end up sleeping with the fishes.

We chaperones had already gotten into enough trouble
at the baby beluga whale tank, visiting the pride of the New
Haven Aquarium and star of its merch. My best parent pals,
and a bunch of others, were shepherding two busloads of first
graders through the maze of exhibits. Our group had reached
the viewing area, watching the pudgy white whale wheel and
twirl through the clear blue water.

The kids were oohing and aahing, still young enough that
they didn't need to play it cool, so we grown-ups could let ourselves be awed too. My friend Corinna and I were enjoying the
scene and the reactions of our kids, my Daniel and her Cherise,
when the whale seemed to pause, treading water for a moment
and looking as uncomfortable as a floating sea creature could.
Then, there was an eddy in the water on its underside, and the
whale's face seemed to relax.

I didn't get it until a little voice from the back piped up:

"Look, Mommy, the whale's peeing!"

The guide, the kids, and most of the parents dissolved into laughter.

For its part, the now-relieved whale just twirled away, back to its rounds.

"Stop that, Jaden!" snapped a brittle female voice in response to little-boy giggles. "Don't be vulgar!"

"Aw, c'mon, Kryssie," I said. "It's a whale. They don't need bathrooms."

"We don't have to *talk* about it," huffed the president of the PTA, as Corinna sent me a sympathetic eye roll.

I sighed. No point in arguing.

"And you people could do a better job of keeping track of your exhibits," Kryssie continued, turning on our guide, ruining the moment for him too.

"Well, ma'am," he said, in an impressively cool tone for a beleaguered college student, "whales are mammals. And mammals urinate."

Unfortunately, his wireless mic was on, and the key word echoed throughout the exhibit.

Kids giggled. So did their parents.

Except one.

"Really!" Kryssie snapped. "I want to talk to your supervisor!"

The guy took a moment to disconnect his mic.

And the Sea Otter Express saved his bacon.

As Kryssie wound up for a big confrontation, the choo-choo whistle of the mini-train that ran through the aquarium sounded, and the clackety-clack started on the track above the whale tank. Everyone looked up to watch the cute turquoise locomotive and the open dark-blue cars decorated with all kinds of sea creatures trundling along the track. Our group's tour had started with a spin, so I knew the track over the tank was actually very safe, even if it looked pretty thrilling.

The ride was a real highlight of the aquarium trip, and I was sure everyone on the train was having as much fun as our group had, with the expansive view of the tank and the whale—and the currently giggling crowd. Too bad the tour only included one ride.

Suddenly, above the clackety-clack came a yell from the far side of the train, followed by a loud grunt and an almighty splash...

That sure wasn't part of the tour.

Parents and kids shrank back from the tank, everyone grabbing whichever children were closest while keeping eyes on their own. Screams and sobs started to filter down from the train above, and I looked up to see my pal Brian and his boyfriend, Pete, in the crowd of riders staring down at the scene in stunned horror.

Inside the tank, the whale was visible only as a white shadow at the far end. Aquatic biologists are right—whales really are smart.

Closer to the front, the tank's new addition was clearly visible: a chunky guy in his thirties, who was immediately recognizable by his Notre Dame sweatshirt. We don't get a lot of Fighting Irish fans around here.

He wasn't moving. Unconscious or dead, I couldn't say.

My money was on dead, though.

And that was a problem.

Because *I* was supposed to kill him.

CHAPTER TWO
AFTER THE WAVE

"Well, what are you going to do about this?" Kryssie asked the guide. "I hope you know these children are now traumatized and our day is ruined."

"Ma'am…" he tried.

"You'll be hearing from our lawyers!"

Uh-oh.

Under their thick fringe of lash extensions, Kryssie's eyes sharpened on me. "Grace! You're a lawyer. Tell these people…"

I looked at the kid. "As an officer of the court, I have only one thing to say to you."

He met my gaze with wide, worried eyes.

"Call nine-one-one, and worry about us later."

Kryssie wheeled on me. "Grace!"

"Speaking of lawyers, Kryssie…as you so accurately observed, I am one, and I'm aware of a little thing called duty of care. That fella in the water is under the care of this place, and our friend here is responsible for him at some level."

"He's responsible for us too!" she huffed.

"Yes, but we're not in imminent danger."

"And being unconscious at the bottom of a whale tank pretty much qualifies as imminent danger," Corinna added.

"What do you know?" Kryssie snapped. "You're a librarian."

"Who is also responsible for the people at my facility." She nodded to the guy, who had stepped away and started dialing. "And he's doing the only right thing, legally—or, as it happens, morally."

"Oh, fine. What do we do?"

I shrugged and looked at the kids, who'd escaped from their adult handlers so they could stare at the tank as if it were a TV screen. "Well, we might want to get the kids away from the tank."

Kryssie let out a squawky shriek of horror, and she immediately started flapping over to her son, practically taking out the Majeskie twins on her way.

Corinna and I exchanged glances and waded into the crowd. As far as we could tell, other than Kryssie's son, who looked pretty scared because he thought his mom was angry with him, the rest of the cherubs didn't seem especially traumatized.

So far.

Thankfully, they were young enough that they were probably processing it as if it were a cartoon. Not the real and unpleasant end of a person they slightly knew.

Actually, even though I had recognized the Notre Dame sweatshirt, the kids in the tank area may not have even realized he was with our group. The man had landed face down, and from our end of the display, all we could see was a bulky, dark-haired form, and the word "Irish" across the back of the sweatshirt.

As Corinna and I herded kids, I thought about the victim. Eric Egan was the elementary curriculum consultant for the school district, some kind of minor mid-level functionary. He wasn't a teacher or a school employee, but worked for a private company helping the district improve the curriculum. For a nice price. We occasionally saw him hanging around the building or sitting in the back of a classroom, and like everyone else with any connection to Rowland Elementary, he got drafted to help with big events like field trips.

He didn't have a lot to do with the kids, which was a very good thing.

Because that's where I came in.

Eric Egan was not marked for removal because of his efforts to replace phonics with sight reading. The problem was his former life, as the junior pastor and enabler of a predatory priest in New Jersey. The client, known to me only as the father of a victim—because confidentiality is all—had paid an appropriately significant sum to my ancient order of lady poisoners, and I had been assigned to carry out the commission.

While the documentation on Eric Egan was rather thin, there was no doubt he met the criteria. Testimony in a number of survivor lawsuits made it clear he'd lured unsuspecting boys to the predator, promising homework help, or video games, or just time with a man they looked up to. Of course, he'd preyed on the most vulnerable boys, and of course the damage was incalculable. The predator himself was conveniently dead—not, as far as I knew, with any help from my sisters—leaving only Egan. As the Church has done brilliantly, and nefariously, for the last couple of thousand years, the prelates swept Egan up and dumped him in a new place. They made it seem like he'd chosen to move on, when they'd really thrown him out and disavowed all responsibility for him.

I didn't doubt whoever came up with the plan assumed Egan would be a paper pusher in an office and never see children. I also didn't doubt they never gave him another thought once he was gone from their sight.

Unlike his victims and their families.

Which ultimately led to me and my sisters.

We've been around for the last seven hundred years or so, hiding in plain sight and ready to set things right when man's justice fails. Any time an evil man drops dead at a particularly convenient or especially appropriate time, we might be involved. Over the centuries, my sisters have removed a fair number of princes, prelates, pirates, and yes, even a president or two. Much of my career, unfortunately, has involved predatory priests or their helpers, so Egan was, very depressingly for the mother of a boy, right in my wheelhouse.

We consider ourselves sacred to the Archangel Gabriel, but as far as I know, none of us have ever met Them—angels do not have gender in our limited human sense. It's really a lot like the church women's group: We believe in the unseen, we follow our faith, and we do good works.

Though, of course, our good work is murder for hire.

While we have an iron ethical code, we exist for the very purpose of defending the vulnerable, so I had been entirely within my rights when I quietly tipped off my friends that they should never allow Eric Egan near their children. They know I sometimes learn confidential information as a lawyer, and they were smart enough not to ask for details—not that I could have offered any.

They were also smart enough to even more quietly pass on the same info to anyone else who might listen, always as a subtle, unattributed caution, which would be more than enough for most sensible people.

And anyway, Eric Egan was not going to be a problem for long.

The aquarium trip was far too high-profile a time to strike, however, and I'd been using the day merely to get a sense of the man, while keeping a close eye on him. It had been reassuring to know he was in Brian and Pete's group, because they're as fierce and protective as they come. And while I didn't know details, I'd picked up a vibe from Pete one day when we were talking about a famous abuse case in the news.

There was no doubt in my mind that Egan would have had to pass through either or both of them to victimize any child.

I also had no doubt that they would never have gone after him in the presence of Brian's daughter Zooey—unless they had absolutely no choice.

Just then, the train engine wheezed to life, and a voice on the loudspeaker urged everyone to stay seated and keep their hands in the cars. We all looked up sharply at the sound, and I saw Brian and Pete in the back car, surrounded by kids, stunned, but clearly keeping watch.

The first car was empty. I could just see the outline of the far door, off-kilter as if it had been jammed back into place. Maybe the train attendant did it after Egan fell, to secure it?

Somebody must have herded everyone into the other two cars. It might be important to know where Brian and Pete were, if only to clear them.

Why was I assuming this wasn't just an unfortunate accident? Because it was happening in my world, of course.

Not that this was the moment to process anything. Corinna and I, and even Kryssie, spent the next several minutes gently moving the kids away from the tank and trying to keep them from looking too closely at the scene. For all the good it did.

"Ma!" Daniel pulled on my sleeve when I reached him, his eyes wide behind his glasses, looking more than usual like a redheaded baby owl. "Is the whale going to eat the guy?"

"I don't think so, sweetheart," I said, keeping my voice as smooth and cool as I could. "I'm pretty sure they only eat fish."

"Well, he's lying there like a dead fish," observed Jake, a tiny blond boy who'd been trying to run away for most of the trip.

"Don't look, Jakie," called a puffy, tired-looking older man a few steps behind him.

"Fine, Pop."

Corinna and I exchanged eye rolls over the kids' heads and kept herding our charges toward the other end of the enclosure. If she weren't one of my best friends, I'd have envied the way her spice-red lipstick perfectly picked up her coat, warming her deep skin and emphasizing her regal elegance, even on this trying day.

Ugh, JakesPop. I'd thought Jake and his grandpa were in the group up top. But now I saw a couple of others walking down. So we were probably stuck with JakesPop, blast it. I'd been relieved we wouldn't have to deal with the oldster during the tour.

Not because of his age, but because of his general uselessness.

JakesPop—the only name we had for the fellow, the way casual school acquaintances know me as DanielsMom—was apparently his family's designated standard-bearer for school events. We'd seen the mom and dad at open house, but JakesPop was the one who showed up at classroom parent days and such. And he really wasn't much help, rarely engaging with the rest of us and only pitching in when asked. On field trips, he did a mediocre job of chaperoning Jake and barely acknowledged the other kids, though he was occasionally good for grabbing a bolter back from the curb.

At that exact moment, we had far more important things to worry about than JakesPop.

"What a mess!" Brian said, as he and Pete helped guide Zooey and their other charges back to the lower level. They both had a stunned, shaken expression.

I supposed we did too.

"Worse for you, I'm guessing," I said.

"Are all of you okay?" asked Corinna.

"Yeah." Pete shook his head. "I didn't realize how dangerous the thing was until the guy fell."

"Horrible accident," Corinna said a little too firmly.

"I didn't see anything," Brian replied, without any prompting.

"We were with Zooey," Pete added, "and we just heard a grunt and looked up...and the door was open."

There was more to it than that, I was sure. But this wasn't the time.

The next half-hour or so was a whirlwind, as the rescue squad—and police marine unit—arrived to fish out the victim, and a couple of harried uniformed officers made Kryssie's day by asking her for the chaperone contact list. They clearly weren't interested in corralling and interviewing a bunch of six-year-olds and their worried parents, and if it happened to convince Kryssie that she was indeed the most important person in the room, well, okay.

Honestly, I think they wanted us out of there, and I couldn't blame them.

We were all just as glad to go anyway—more than happy to trade a later call from the New Haven Police for freedom now. The kids were surprisingly subdued and easily herded, and far earlier than expected, we piled onto the buses for home.

Not quite the learning experience we'd planned.

CHAPTER THREE
RESCUE ME

The caravan had just crossed into Alcott when my phone buzzed with a text.

Need some help. Call me ASAP.

From Al Kaufman, the fiancé of my good friend and handler, Madge Arsenault. *What on earth?*

What? I replied.

Vince Scupper and I got arrested. We need a lawyer. Can you get here?

Sure. Will park Daniel with his pals and get to you in an hour or so.

Thanks.

Far easier said than done, but it had to be dire if Al, a retired police detective, and Vince, a senior assistant state's attorney—and my former mentor—had managed to get themselves arrested.

And I wasn't even the one with the worst mess. Corinna had to get back to the library because a simmering donnybrook over a book about two boy penguins raising a chick was about to blow. It was her first big controversy as library director, and she had to smack the book-banners down fast and hard.

With all that going on, Brian and Pete took the kids, promising an afternoon at the hardware store, with the added draw of story time with Old Man Loquat, Brian's nearly 100-year-old great-uncle, who could always be counted upon for a thrilling World War II tale.

We couldn't have planned a better way for the kids to decompress after the trip.

A few minutes after one, I snagged the only remaining visitor space at the New Haven police station and headed to the front desk, walking briskly but not running, because a worried rush is a bad look for a defense lawyer. Not that I looked much like a lawyer. Fortunately, it wasn't an especially cold day, and I'd worn my calf-length black trench coat. As long as I kept it buttoned, nobody would see my mom-standard skinny pants, royal-blue waterfall cardigan, and fun seahorse-print tee. I was stuck with the lug-sole Mary Janes.

Ugh.

Can't help it now. As I approached the front desk, I drew myself up to my full height and squared my shoulders into confident court posture, then pulled my face into a friendly yet respectful smile for the sergeant.

"Hello, Sergeant Ramsay," I said, taking note of the desk nameplate. "I'm Grace Adair, lawyer for Al Kaufman and Vince Scupper."

The sergeant smiled, and I recognized her—and she me.

"Well, how about that. Good for you, Grace. I'm glad they called you."

We chuckled together.

"Sharon," I said. "Glad you finally got out of records."

"Glad you finally got out of the station wagon."

When I first met Sergeant Sharon Ramsay, she'd been running the records room while recovering from an IED blast on a National Guard deployment in Iraq. She wasn't thrilled with being inside, and I wasn't thrilled with all the research required of a junior assistant state's attorney. Her recovery took a lot longer than my rise in the state's attorney's office, and I'd seen her occasionally during my years there. The last time I'd seen her, she'd been in records again—but that time was owing to her being in the late stages of a pregnancy, just as I'd been at the time.

"So, how is she?" I asked.

"Beautiful, wonderful, and driving me nuts. Yours?"

"He's about the same. Pics?"

"Plenty. Catch me after you talk to the fellas. They've been chewing on my shoes for the last half hour demanding to know when their lawyer would get here."

"Sorry. Had to finish a field trip."

Sharon's gaze sharpened. "You were with the aquarium group?"

"Yeah. Big mess."

"Bigger than you think. You should expect to hear from one of the detectives."

"It's not an accident?"

"Looks like there's a lot going on there."

"Great." I shook my head. "Well, I'll be glad to tell them what I saw. Right now, I'd better find out what's going on with the gentlemen."

"It's a weird one, Grace."

"Weird how?"

"They got brought in on a stalking charge."

"Stalking?"

"Yeah. Neighborhood patrol got a call of two old men staking out some guy's house…and when they went to check it, there they were."

"This is really out of character." I shook my head. "Thanks. Talk soon."

"Absolutely." She buzzed me in, nodded toward the hallway as her face and voice took on a serious, professional air. The social part of our program was over. "They're in the lieu's office. Nobody thought it was a good idea to send them to holding."

"Thank you for that." I nodded to her and started down the hall.

Even if I hadn't seen the sign for Lieutenant C. Luciano's

office, I would have been able to find them by the sound of the argument.

"Why didn't you tell the beat cops to leave us alone?" Vince.

"The job isn't a free pass now," Al snapped back. "Even I know that. And I'm not on the street anymore."

"Good thing. As slow as you move, you'd—"

I knocked. Loudly. "Gentlemen?"

A beleaguered-looking young male officer opened the door. "Are you the lawyer?"

"I am."

"Oh, good!" His big blue eyes widened in relief. "Um, I mean—"

"It's fine, Officer." I gave him a reassuring smile—because a pat on the head would have been inappropriate—and stepped inside.

Two adorable old men turned to me.

Al was fit and balding, and instead of his usual getup of brown suede jacket, Yale sweatshirt, and jeans, he had on a rumpled Columbo-style trench coat over khakis. Not, I was sure, a coincidence.

Opposite him, in a three-piece gray court suit that didn't quite hide his little cannoli tummy, a faint mussing of his white mane the only sign of trouble, was my old mentor in the state's attorney's office, senior prosecutor Vince.

Both were standup guys, ethical to a fault, and had spent a lifetime upholding the law. So what on earth were they doing on the wrong side of it?

"Grace, finally!" Al exclaimed.

"About time you got here, MacInnes," Vince growled. While many of my colleagues address each other by last names, Vince only used my maiden name when he was annoyed. It was his tell.

Good for both of them. Considering everything I'd had to juggle to get here, I wasn't interested in their feelings.

"As your attorney, I do not want to know how you got arrested for stalking until we are in a secure, confidential environment," I said by way of greeting.

They drooped like bad little boys.

I turned to the young cop, checking his tag. "So, Officer Hennessey, can we just write up appearance tickets for these two?"

"I'm sorry, but they're supposed to go to arraignment court."

"Really?" I asked. "They wrote it up as felony stalking?"

"Let me get the lieutenant," he said, quickly stepping out the door.

As he opened the door, a slim woman with wine-red lipstick and salt-and-pepper hair pulled back in a smooth cop bun appeared. Her well-cut black suit and burgundy crepe blouse were just a bit nicer than you'd expect for police brass, which was probably the point.

"Ms. Adair?" she asked in a tone silky enough for a trial lawyer.

"Yes. Grace. I was MacInnes when I was a prosecutor." I held out my hand. "Lieutenant Luciano?"

"Carla." She smiled and shook. "I think we may have met when I did crowd control on a few scenes back in the day."

"Probably."

I put my hands in my pockets, and she folded her arms.

"So," I said, "what happened here?"

"Well, these two fellows have apparently been spending a lot of time parked in front of Ethan Storey's house. And Mr. Storey finally called the neighborhood precinct today."

"Ethan Storey?"

"He's scum," Al said.

"Creep," added Vince.

"He is, at this exact moment," said Lieutenant Luciano, "our victim, and you would do well to remember that."

More squirmy, unhappy little-boy faces.

"The name is familiar," I said, "but I don't remember why."

"He was one of the teens convicted in the Cathie Holman case," said the lieutenant.

I managed not to gasp.

Just over two decades ago, fourteen-year-old Cathie Holman had been lured to a deserted lakeside park by a group of teenagers and beaten within an inch of her life. It was an infamous bullying incident and led to a series of school and criminal-justice reforms, not least because all six participants got relatively short sentences thanks to their age and the fact that Cathie Holman survived. At least physically.

I hadn't known Al was involved in the Holman case. For Vince, it had long been an open wound, and I remembered him insisting on charging some young offenders as adults—or filing more serious charges—to prevent a repeat of what he saw as a major injustice. To Vince's way of thinking, Cathie Holman's attackers deserved to spend the rest of their lives in jail because they'd taken the life she would have had.

I didn't completely disagree. But I also know teenagers don't understand the permanence of their actions the way adults do and may deserve some level of mercy.

"I see," I said as coolly as I could.

"Storey wants to press charges," the lieutenant said, fixing a glare on the guys. "And while I'm not crazy about hauling a decorated detective and a legendary prosecutor off to the lockup..."

"You can't just brush off the behavior," I said.

"Exactly."

We nodded together.

There was a long pause while Carla Luciano continued to glare at Al and Vince.

Then she nodded to them, and spoke:

"I don't think it helps anyone to send these two to arraignment court. If the charges are written up as misdemeanor trespassing, they'll still have to answer them, but they won't have to be processed."

"Desk appearance ticket?" I asked. "With the understanding that any repeats will not be handled so indulgently."

"I think that'll work, don't you, gentlemen?"

They gave grudging shrugs. The lieutenant's expression suggested she wasn't sold.

"C'mon, fellas," I urged. "I think Lieutenant Luciano is waiting for you to give her your word."

They exchanged glances, then shook their heads at me.

"Do you *want* to go to the lockup?" I asked.

Two reluctant sighs.

"We won't harass him again," Vince said.

"No stalking," added Al.

The lieutenant studied them for another long, uncomfortable moment, then took a deep breath. "All right. Go forth and sin no more."

"Thank you, Lieutenant," I said. "I'll have a good talk with them."

"Thank you, Grace." A faint smile. "And it's still Carla."

Shared nods.

I shepherded the guys out, but not before very deliberately taking two minutes to exchange kid pics and chatter with Sergeant Ramsay. Important to keep the friendship—and to put my charges in their place.

Anyone who knows anything about the court system will tell you the whole process of delay and deliberation is part of the punishment.

Outside, I nodded to my car. "I'll get you home, but we're taking the long way so you two jokers can explain to me how we got here."

"How about we buy you coffee and a cannoli?" offered Vince.

"And some cookies for your fellas?" added Al.

"I think I can find an hour for you—and some good cookies." I clicked the locks. "Get in."

CHAPTER FOUR
TAKE THE CANNOLI

E rsalesi's Bakery is where the smart locals go for their cannoli. There are better-known spots with fancy social media
presence, but nobody has tastier or fresher pastries or smoother
coffee. It's a madhouse in the morning and early evening, but
they usually have a midafternoon lull, and we were lucky
enough to hit just at the end of it.

Within a few minutes, the three of us were seated at a small
table toward the back, with a paper plate of cannoli in the center, to-go boxes for later, and cups of that rich Italian roast.

Black, of course. Serious people do not do business over
fancy beverages. Even if we're enjoying Ersalesi's cannoli.

Not that we were touching the pastries—yet.

We needed the coffee first. Probably for different reasons,
but each of us did.

The guys buried their faces in the cups, whether for the revi-
talizing scent of the steam or as a convenient hiding place, I
didn't know. I was too busy getting my own coffee boost.

"Damn, that's good stuff," Vince said finally, putting down his cup.

"Got that," Al agreed.

"No argument there." I took one more precious sip before we got down to business.

Vince and Al watched me place my cup on the table.

The simple fact they were letting me take the lead meant they knew how bad it was.

"All right," I said. "Do you want to tell me how we got here?"

"Storey belongs in jail," snarled Vince.

"Sooner or later, he'll get himself sent back," added Al.

"And you two are going to make sure of it." I sighed. "Does this have something to do with the twenty years since?"

Both gave ambiguous shrugs.

There had been a follow-up story a few months ago, and a TV reporter had tried to track down everyone involved. Ethan Storey was the only one they'd been able to find, and he'd refused to speak. So the story had been heavy on the details from the original incident, more than lurid enough to remind a couple of old stand-up guys of what they saw as an unpaid debt.

"How long have you been following him?" I asked.

"Not long enough," said Al.

"Creeps don't change." Vince picked up a cannoli and snapped off a bite like a shark with its prey. For a moment, the transcendent taste softened his expression. "Even my mother, God rest her, couldn't make cannoli like this."

Al reached for one. "Definitely tops Bubbe's teiglach."

"What?" I asked. My friend Brian made *his* bubbe's rugelach and kugel, but I'd never heard him refer to this.

"Nasty little balls of dough, coated in sugar so you'll crack your teeth on 'em." Al broke off an edge of the cannoli and scooped out a dab of cream.

"Like Mom's struffoli," Vince said. "Woman was a saint, but every Christmas she tried to kill us. It's kind of like one of these cream-puff towers, only the balls are tiny and there's no cream. They're usually like rocks. But the Ersalesi's do a good one—my daughter had it for her rehearsal dinner."

"We're doing the cream-puff tower for the Viennese table,"

Al said. "Goes with the chocolate fountain."

"You're having the chocolate fountain?" Vince asked. "I love those. But don't waste money on the fruit plate. Nobody eats it."

"Good point. I thought maybe strawberries," said Al.

"Maybe in the summer when they're cheap." Vince took another bite of cannoli. "But don't even bother in the winter. All anyone really wants are the cream puffs, the little brownies, and the pound cake."

"Brownies?" Al asked, taking a bite of his pastry. "I need to make sure they put those out."

"Oh, yeah." Vince nodded as he took a sip of coffee. "Gotta dip the brownies."

They were warming to the topic, which admittedly made a good diversion, and I strongly suspected they were hoping to time me out. After all, I had to get back to Alcott to scoop up Daniel in time for homework and dinner—to say nothing of getting our giant dog, Scotchie, out for a walk.

"All right. We're all in favor of brownies," I said. "Now back to Ethan Storey."

"I'd rather talk brownies, honestly," Vince said.

"Yeah." Al nodded. "At least that's fun."

"The brownies," I said pointedly, "did not just pick you up at the police station."

Both tried to glare at me.

I glared back and picked up my cannoli, taking a small bite off the end.

Whatever else happened that day, the sheer delight of the pastry did make up for a lot. As soon as I finished the bite, though, I returned to the laser glare.

"All right, so you know Ethan Storey was one of the six kids who attacked Cathie Holman." Vince tried to keep a clinical tone, but didn't quite make it.

"He said he didn't participate," Al said. "But he still should have gotten twenty for hiding in the bushes and not getting help."

"They all should have gotten life," Vince spat. "Or sentences stacked so it amounted to it."

We could have been there all night refighting the case, and I definitely did not have time for it. "We know the justice system didn't do well here. But why were you at his house today?"

"It's twenty years since it happened. We saw the piece on TV. He shouldn't just be running around out there." Al put down his cannoli with a scowl.

"And nobody but us seems to care," said Vince.

"So you're hoping…"

"He's got to be up to something dirty," Al said.

"Has to. Leopards don't change their spots," agreed Vince.

"Is he the only one left?" I didn't remember details, the way things get lost in the busy years of early parent life, but I thought all—or most—of the attackers had died in various unfortunate ways.

"The only one we can find," Al said.

"The girls involved in the attack are dead," Vince confirmed. "You know about Cade MacAvoy—the murder-suicide."

I nodded, as the name tripped a few memories. "Right."

"Even though he was an adult, Storey got a shorter sentence and long probation because he cooperated," Al said. "And he stayed around."

"Should have dropped off the end of the earth," Vince spat. "Like the other one."

"Doremus." Al pronounced the name like it was a byword for evil. "Youngest kid. Egged them on. And he basically got away with it."

"He did?"

"Served his sentence in juvie and disappeared. Probably out there somewhere with a different name." Vince picked up his cannoli and took an angry bite. "Some bleeding-heart group probably took him up and gave him a new start."

"Not like anybody was racing out to do that for poor Cathie."

"Do you know…" I asked.

"Lost touch a while ago." Al shrugged. "Didn't want to intrude."

I nodded. I understood that.

"I know she's alive," Vince said. "Got an alert on her record. Beyond that, I don't know anything."

"And the Doremus kid?"

"Can't even do an alert on him," Vince replied. "Must have changed his social security number—which people can do if they get special permission."

"Not that he deserved it."

I caught a glimpse of the clock out of the corner of my eye. As much as I wanted to explore the aftermath of the case—and the potential whereabouts of Ronald Doremus—I had to get back to Alcott.

"All right," I said. "You have to stop chasing Ethan Storey. Now that you've been charged, it's not going to get better."

Both of them glared at me.

"And you know I'm right."

"Oh, fine, Grace." Al sighed. "Okay."

"You gave Lieutenant Luciano your word, and I want the same."

They drooped and scowled like misbehaving little boys.

"I mean it."

For a long moment, I gave them my very best mom glare, which works wonders with Daniel. These two were much tougher cases—but both had had formidable mothers, and I hoped it would work.

They mumbled assent.

It would have to do.

And—with the clock ticking—I would have to take the cannoli.

CHAPTER FIVE
HARDWARE AND HARD TALKS

I dropped Vince and Al off at Vince's apartment complex, a few blocks from Ersalesi's. My guess was they'd been using Vince's place as home base, since Al lived in Alcott. Not to mention being in the middle of the wedding whirlwind.

By then, it was heading for four, and I had to take a couple of obscure little back road shortcuts to return to Alcott without getting stuck in early-rush traffic. I wanted to scoop up Daniel and head home to Scotchie before I faced an entirely different kind of scooping.

At Loquat's Hardware, I started up the walk from the parking lot just as Corinna crossed from the library, her bright red coat standing out in the waning winter light. We started laughing at the sight of each other and met up at the foot of the porch stairs.

"How go the wars?" I asked.

"Not bad. The angry grandma read the book, and decided she doesn't need to get her information from social media next time."

"That'll work."

"Now we just need the rest of them to start using their brains instead of their feeds." Corinna sighed. "What about you? Everyone okay?"

"Yeah." I'd pleaded unspecified legal emergency, knowing my friends understood the confidentiality issues. "Had to bail out a client who got themselves arrested for something stupid. Michael's in court today so he couldn't do it."

"Grandma was right. You can't fix stupid."

"My grandpa said that too."

We shared a smile as I opened the door, and she walked through.

Inside, we were greeted by a warm and wonderful scene.

Happy customers were wandering through the aisles as usual, but the focus was at the store stove, a real nineteenth-century cast-iron treasure, probably the original one from the store opening in the 1870s. And at the stove, in an equally vintage rocking chair, the living treasure of the place: Old Man Loquat.

Loquat's Hardware had been at this spot for about a century and a half, and for most of that time, the eldest male in the clan had been known as Old Man Loquat, a title of respect equal to anything on offer at the Court of St. James. The current incumbent was a World War II veteran, great-uncle to my friend Brian Stein. When Brian inherited his grandmother's share of the business, neither of them had been sure how it would work out. Brian didn't know if the old-school fella would be comfortable in business with him—and the patriarch wasn't sure a widowed gay ad copywriter from New York would fit in Alcott.

But Old Man Loquat would be the first to tell you it wasn't "the gay thing" because he didn't fight a war against bigots to become one. It was the small-town life thing, and that was much bigger than who somebody loves.

As it turned out, though, Brian shared Old Man Loquat's sense for customers and had handyman skills honed by a fixer-upper apartment in Brooklyn. Better, the two bonded over their shared loneliness as widowers—and mutual adoration of Brian's daughter, Zooey. Now the three were an unlikely and very happy blended family, and the hardware store was doing better than ever.

All good.

Today, as he often did on cold winter afternoons, Old Man Loquat was telling stories, with the store cat, Jimmy Stewart, curled up in his lap. There'd been a store cat by that name since at least the 1930s. The current edition was a regal calico who had very little use for anyone who was not her person, but would occasionally tolerate a pet from the children, if they were careful and gentle.

The kids, of course, lived in hope of this, and watched the kitty for any sign that today was the day. She'd never scratched any of them, but she had been known to hiss—or snort and flounce away—if she smelled another animal on them. Today's odds were probably better than usual, since the kids had been at the aquarium and far away from their respective pets.

"Hey, Corinna—and Gracie!" Old Man Loquat greeted us with a big smile—and the nickname only he was permitted to use. I liked it coming from him.

"Hi there!" we called back.

Both of us stopped and gave our kids a pat and a quickly-brushed-off kiss on top of the head as we moved toward the old man. It had been too much of a day to not need the first little bit of contact.

When we reached the rocking chair and shook hands, Jimmy Stewart shot glares at us, but didn't move. She was too content with her person—and the stove.

"Glad to see you two," he said, and then nodded to the kids. "Why don't you three go see if Brian remembered to unbox some more treats for Jimmy?"

The kids trooped off, and the old man looked at us. "Keep an eye on them tonight, huh?"

"Oh?" Corinna and I asked in unintended unison.

"This kind of thing can be really upsetting for young kids. My little sister happened to be standing on the platform when a man jumped in front of a train. She was never the same, and I always thought it was because we didn't talk about it right after. We didn't back then, you know."

For a moment, I was a little startled, and then I realized it was classic Old Man Loquat. Always determined to share the lessons of his long life.

"Thank you," I said.

"Good advice," added Corinna. "We'll talk it through this evening."

"Us too," I agreed. "You're right, sir, it's always better to process things openly and early."

Just about everyone called Old Man Loquat "sir." It would be unimaginable not to use the honorific.

"Figured you would. You aren't going to go nuts like some of those folks—but kids see more than you think they do, and they may need a little extra care and feeding for a bit." The old man gave us a smile. "You're smart ladies, but probably just a little overwhelmed today."

"Oh, a little," I said. "Legal stuff."

"And a book protest. Solved that, though."

"Good. People should read any damn thing they like—sorry ladies."

"We agree," Corinna said.

"Nothing good ever starts with a book burning," said Old Man Loquat, who knew better than most.

"True that," I said.

"No argument there." Corinna looked at him and the cat. "How's your book supply, sir? There's a brand-new account of the Battle of the Marne, based on new studies at the scene, if you'd like me to bring it over tomorrow."

Since the old fella was a World War I buff, Corinna had found her mark. His eyes gleamed with curiosity. "Yes, please."

"Will do. And maybe Jimmy will let me pet her if I'm not wearing a sweater with another cat's hair."

"Better luck than me," I said. "I smell like a giant dog."

"Not to us, thankfully," Corinna said.

The old man laughed. "That's not a dog. It's the hound of the Baskervilles. Just nicer."

"Much nicer," I agreed.

"Does somebody need cat treats?"

Pete Hurley walked up holding a bag of Kitty Greenies, the kids a few steps behind him.

Pete, a tall, strawberry-blond landscape architect, moved to town last year to take care of his ailing father and recover from a nasty divorce. His ex-husband had sold their waterside house right out from under him and moved west. When he arrived in Alcott, he was raw, wounded, and sure he'd never get another chance at love and a family.

And then he showed up in the hardware store and found another cautious, lonely soul behind the counter. With a little shove from the cast—especially Old Man Loquat, who had enlisted the rest of us to help in his matchmaking efforts—he and Brian had begun a sweet, slow-burn courtship. He'd helped chaperone the aquarium trip as a non-pushy way to be more involved in Zooey's school life with an eye to the long-term.

So far, everything looked good.

"Thanks, Pete," said the old man, taking the bag from him. "Was just telling the ladies the same thing I told you and Brian. Just need to keep watch on the kids."

"And we will, for sure, sir." Pete nodded and turned to us. "How are you two holding up? I don't envy you having to jump back into the day after that."

"Part of the deal," Corinna said. "When you're the director, there's always something."

"And somebody always needs a lawyer," I added. "But I sure won't be sorry when wine o'clock comes."

"Think it's going to be limoncello o'clock at my house," Corinna said. "Got a bottle of that nice locally made stuff."

"I was thinking cocoa and a bad movie," Pete said with a sheepish shrug. "I don't need any nightmares from the alcohol."

"I don't know," Brian added as he walked over from the counter, his amiable round face tight and troubled. "Might take my chances on tequila."

"Nonsense," said the old man as he opened the treat bag and the cat's head went up. "You drink an inch of Scotch at the end of the day, talk a little, cry if you need to, sleep off the worst of it, and keep walking tomorrow."

As the kids closed in, we grownups exchanged nods.

There were a lot worse ways to handle this.

CHAPTER SIX
DINNER AND DRAMA

Dinnertime was, no surprise, a scramble. We dashed home and got Scotchie out just in time for that much-needed walk—let's just say we managed to avoid at least one environmental disaster that day. Daniel buckled down to do his homework while I started dinner. Days ago, I'd been smart enough to make and freeze a nice casserole so I wouldn't hear my husband Michael's whining about my usual go-to dish on busy days.

For some reason, Michael had a continued vendetta against my quick-and-dirty chicken parmigiana, made from frozen cutlets and jarred sauce, and I'd assumed I wouldn't want that battle after a day of shepherding kids around the aquarium.

Little did I know.

Michael, who was finishing a long and difficult plea agreement negotiation, blew in just in time to bring the salad to the table while Daniel set out the silverware. He tries to pitch in and make sure Daniel does too, with an eye to Daniel's future partner.

For someone who can be pretty darn clueless with *his* partner, Michael is awfully good about teaching his son to be an excellent spouse. Of course, watching my fellas warmed my heart: Daniel, with his bright smile and tufted red hair, is a miniature copy of his dad.

After he set the salad bowl on the table, Michael came back into the kitchen to pick up plates and stopped to watch as I peeled the foil off the casserole.

Even just doing ordinary routine home stuff, it was good to look up and see Michael. Not just because he's gorgeous, though the friends who joked about his resemblance to the guy from *Outlander* aren't entirely wrong. No, what's really important is, no matter how busy we are, our eyes meet and we feel the bond, strong as ever.

"Tough day, Tweety. You okay?"

He started using the nickname shortly after we began dating, a reference, as he put it at the time, to my big blue eyes. The sweetness of it always melted me at least a little.

"Yeah," I agreed, with an embarrassing wobble in my voice.

"C'mere." He pulled me into an embrace, and I leaned on him for a moment. Michael's an inch or so taller than me and muscular, and he hugs like anyone who wants you is going to have to come through him.

It was an awfully soothing feeling after a stressful day.

I burrowed into his embrace for a moment, enjoying the warmth, and the faint scent of aftershave. Damn.

"You know," I said, pulling back enough to give him a kiss on the cheek. "I am a very lucky woman."

"I'm a lucky man." He grinned. "Maybe we'll really be lucky and have some energy left at the end of the day."

"We can only hope."

"Ma! Scotchie ate my napkin!"

Michael let go of me and dashed back into the dining room, where yes, our giant blond mutt had indeed taken an appetizer. Fortunately, it was a paper napkin, so there were unlikely to be any serious consequences. Unfortunately, it was a bright blue one, which meant there might well be unpleasantness for whoever took Scotchie out tomorrow.

But that was tomorrow.

After dinner, I was loading the dishwasher while Michael helped Daniel with his reading homework when my phone buzzed.

A text from Madge: **Call me. Now.**

Not a surprise. I figured my handler would want to talk to me since my commission had just disappeared in a splash.

With a quick wave to Michael, I grabbed the laundry hamper and headed downstairs. Plenty of space for a chat. As soon as I threw in the clothes and hit the button, I dialed. It couldn't have been more than a minute.

Too long for Madge.

"We have a big problem." No greeting, no nothing. And a voice brittle with fear.

I had to figure she was overreacting because of wedding stress.

"You mean the man who died at the aquarium today?" I asked. "Probably some kind of freak accident. And I've always understood that the commission dies with the subject."

"It does. No refunds." Her voice loosened just a bit. "You'll have to keep an eye on it, but we probably have little or no concern there. At least for now."

"Then what?"

"Al and Vince."

"Oh." I wasn't sure how much she knew. I had no intention of holding out, but I also thought Al should be the one to tell her.

"I know they got arrested. And I know you bailed them out."

"Of course I did," I said. "What else would I do?"

"Let the fools rot in the lockup," she snapped. "This is a disaster."

"It's not ideal," I agreed, "but they're probably going to plead it down to a minor trespassing charge and that'll be the end of it."

"Not quite."

"What? It might—*might*—be a minor issue if Al were looking for security work, but I doubt it'll even be a problem for Vince at the state's attorney's office." Vince had been around so long he was essentially untouchable. And misdemeanor trespassing might or might not even flag on a background check, depending on who was doing it and how.

"It's not work, Grace. It's the Mothers."

"Oh, come on." I let out an exasperated sigh. "If a misdemeanor arrest were disqualifying, a lot of sisters would never marry. You can get a misdemeanor arrest for traffic offenses, for heaven's sake."

"It's not the offense. It's the stalking."

"What do you mean?"

"He's trying to exact his own vengeance." She sighed. "Or at least moving in that direction. If I were Professor Munroe, I'd order me not to marry him."

"Surely not."

"It contradicts all the assurances we've given her. Makes him exactly the sort of man a sister cannot marry."

I wished I could disagree. But I knew the rules. "It's a one-time thing, with one case."

"I know, but still."

I took a breath. Tried to think. "Look. I'm his lawyer, right?"

"Right."

"You call Professor Munroe tonight and tell her what happened. I'll talk to her too and explain that it stops here."

"Can you make it stop here?"

"Well, a lot of that is your job. You've got to make sure Al doesn't keep chasing Ethan Storey."

"I think Al was trying to settle it so he could go into our marriage with a clean slate."

"Look, if I convince Professor Munroe that I can bury it, which I can, you have to make sure it never happens again."

"Or at least until the wedding," Madge said.

"Never. What do you think happens if he gets arrested for chasing Ethan Storey *after* you're married?"

Madge was silent for a moment as the realization hit. "Oh."

"Yeah. So settle it now. It's the only safe way."

"It is, isn't it?"

"To some degree," I said as gently as I could, "jeopardy has already attached."

"Then we've got to fix this."

"And we will." I tried to sound confident. "I'll also tackle Vince, so he's not encouraging Al."

"I think they encourage each other."

"Then we'll have to stop them both."

"Ma!" An insistent little voice from above. "Where are my markers?"

"Oh, hell. Gotta go."

"Okay. I'll do my part tonight."

"And I'll do mine when Professor Munroe calls."

"Hope it's enough."

I didn't have anything to say to that, so I hit End, and dashed upstairs. The next hour or so was a whirlwind, as Daniel finished his homework and Michael holed up in his office to finish his. I returned to an editing project, but honestly, it might as well have been in cuneiform.

We spent a few minutes together tucking in Daniel, as we always do, this time allowing a little extra time for him to talk out what he'd seen and assuring him of his safety. Scotchie helped with the comfort and safety message, draping himself across the bed like a living afghan and snuggling his boy.

After Daniel was down, Michael returned to work, and I just gave up. I took my wine and headed off to bed with a beauty magazine, which was all my brain could handle at that point.

I woke up a while later to find Michael slipping in beside me.

He looked like I felt. Tired, worn out from the events of the day.

But not that tired.

CHAPTER SEVEN
MORNING AFTER BLUES

L et's just say I did not awaken radiant with joy the next day. I was anything but sparkling as I dragged myself through my morning routine, thinking, *I'm tired and I hate everybody.*

Michael bounded up from the basement as I was taking Daniel's French toast sticks out of the microwave.

"Only did ten minutes on the tread, huh?" he asked. He was all glowy from his usual half-hour run at a number-ten incline. Creep.

"Tired from yesterday," I said. *And last night,* I didn't say, dumping a bit too much syrup on Daniel's plate.

"Sticks!" Daniel crowed as I crossed into the dining room.

Back in the kitchen, Michael poured two mugs of coffee while I settled Daniel with his sticks and rewarded Scotchie for letting the kid eat with a slice of Fakin' Bacon.

Michael handed me my I Yell Because I Care mug and rested a hand on my back.

"It was a lot," I admitted, taking a sip. *Not quite as good as*

Ersalesi's, but not bad. "The good news is Daniel and his friends seem to be okay."

"They're young enough that it's not as traumatic as it would be for older kids who really understand what happened."

"Yeah."

"What do you think did happen?"

"I'm still going on the theory it was just a terrible accident," I said. Even I didn't think I sounded convincing.

"Yeah. Okay." Michael took a sip of coffee and held my gaze. "When did you start believing in fairy tales?"

"When I married Prince Charming."

"Ha." He drank a bit more coffee. "Seriously, though, it's a weird way to kill somebody."

"Very weird," I said.

"And what's so special about this man to make somebody want to kill him like that?"

"Good question." I knew a lot more of the answer to that question, but I sure didn't want to get into it. "He was a curriculum guy."

"Curriculum? I thought he was one of the teachers."

"No. Private company paid for by a federal grant—the district got an extra person at each level."

"So, a functionary," Michael said.

"Mostly. He wasn't a classroom guy, but he did show up occasionally at school events, like open house." Which, as it happened, was what led to my involvement. The commission from the Mothers said someone recognized Eric Egan "from his previous life" and decided he had to be permanently kept away from children.

Once I'd run a background check on him, I didn't disagree.

At the very least, I knew Egan was the accomplice of that predatory priest in New Jersey. Despite the best efforts of the retired sisters who investigate potential commissions and the voluminous public record from the lawsuits, there wasn't a lot of detail on where Egan came from or how he ended up in the inner-city Newark parish. Nor any definitive word on whether he had abused those poor, vulnerable boys or simply delivered victims, knowing exactly what would happen to them. For prosecutors, the difference probably mattered. My sisters and I believed the moral violation met the bar.

Honestly, I hadn't been too worried about where Egan came from. My job was to make sure he never went anywhere else. I'd been casing him for a few weeks and had planned to strike soon after the trip. So much for that.

"Well, my money's on an accident." Michael's tone, thankfully, closed the subject, because he was clearly more concerned about the day's other dramatic event. "And you had to bail out Al and Vince?"

"They got pinched for trespassing." I drank more coffee. Sooner or later, it had to start helping.

"Trespassing?" He gave a puzzled glance over the coffee cup.

"Long story. I think they'll be able to plead it down to a fine and probation."

"As long as they stay out of trouble they will." He paused and held eye contact. "Will they?"

"And there, friends, is the rub. I've done my best to convince them, but I have no idea if it'll take."

"Why not?"

Might as well tell him the whole story. He might be able to help. "The guy they're watching is one of the last surviving attackers in the Cathie Holman case."

"Uh-oh." Michael shook his head. "Didn't I see a twenty-year story on TV?"

"You did. I think that sparked it."

"Their case, right?"

"Yeah. And no one came out well: The three girls who were involved are all dead—an overdose, a suspicious single-car crash, and a murder-suicide."

"The murder-suicide involved the guy the whole thing was over, right?"

"Yeah. Cade MacAvoy. And the girl who was the ringleader, Char Torrey. She killed him a month after he got out of prison because he broke up with her." And two weeks after the client who'd hired me to kill MacAvoy called it off. The only time that had ever happened in my career.

Which of course I wouldn't be sharing with Michael.

"Strange poetic justice, I guess," he said.

"Sort of." I took a sip of my coffee. "The whole thing really goes back to the whole weird mid-teens age—everything is heightened, and every slight is life or death. Literally." I paused. "Char Torrey was like the chief Mean Girl, and when poor Cathie drew her boyfriend's attention, Char had to squash her. Obliterate her, really. The others went along because they felt they had to—or else."

"And instead, they ruined their own lives as well as Cathie's."

"Well, we really don't know if Cathie's life is ruined," I said. "We don't know anything about her, really."

"How can you not know?" Michael stared at me. "Nobody *disappears*."

"Well, Vince has an alert on her information, so we know she's alive," I shrugged. "Beyond that, who knows? If I were planning her life, I would have sent her to the other side of the country with a new name."

"Maybe that's what she did."

"I'd like to think so. That she found a happy new life after all of this."

"Even though we all know…"

"Yeah." I sighed. "Very few people recover well from something like that."

"And it's hard to really make it right with a sentence. Didn't they plead to aggravated assault?"

"Most of them did. The youngest guy, Doremus, got juvenile charges. Ethan Storey got assault and long probation because he cooperated."

"And it probably didn't feel like enough to them. Compared to what happened to her."

"You've made the point for me," I said. "Her attackers took whatever life she would have had. Vince and Al thought they should have paid a much higher price."

"How high?" Michael asked.

"Good question." I drank more coffee. "They say they just want the guy to go back to prison. I think I believe them."

"I think you're right." He nodded. "It's not just trusting your judgment, though I do. It's also that these guys have always been by the book, even when the book let them down."

"Exactly. Even in the Gideon Almon case, I think it was Al's partner who killed him," I said. Gideon Almon was a notorious child molester put away by Vince, Al, and Al's late partner, only to be released on a technicality—then found dead of an overdose in his kitchen. While it was possible Al had been the one who did it, I was more inclined to believe his partner, who'd been terminally ill, had settled the score.

Though Al might have known about it.

"That always made the most sense to me." Michael drank the last of his coffee and set down the mug. "I really don't think either of them would go vigilante. But they might get in trouble trying to make sure the system did what they believe to be its job."

"They already have."

"More serious trouble. You need to make it very clear to them this is not going to end well."

"I'm trying to," I said.

"It's not even in the interest of what they hope to accomplish." He grabbed a banana from the fruit bowl and started peeling. "Any evidence they turn up will be questionable."

"I think they're both smart enough to call for backup." I took a breath. "I hope."

"Even so, I know what I'd do if I found out the report on my client had come from one of them."

"Everybody isn't as good as you. Or me."

"This is Defense Lawyering 101." He shrugged. "Any decent lawyer checks how the charges were brought."

"Maybe. Anyhow, you're right. They've got to stop."

"If only because Al needs to get his act together for the wedding."

I chuckled. "He's the groom. There's not all that much for him to do."

"If you're a guy, it's stressful enough to get dressed up and herd your friends to the ceremony."

"Sure it is." I glared. "Madge is currently trying to make a final decision on hair, and what shade of pink the ribbons on the bubble bottles should be."

"What on earth are bubble bottles?"

"Remember how people threw birdseed at us because it's safer than rice?"

"Yeah."

"Well, now, people blow bubbles from teeny-tiny little bottles."

"Of course they do."

"Usually with ribbons on them." His puzzled expression made me laugh. "So don't tell me about poor Al having to get his tuxedo on and make sure his family and friends get to the venue on time."

"Fair enough. Are you still insisting upon being called the flower girl?"

"As I shall be until the end of the ceremony. Madge doesn't want a pack of bridesmaids, and Al's daughter is her matron of honor, so there are only a few things to do with me."

"But an adult woman as…"

This was not the first time we'd had this wrangle.

"An adult woman standing up for her friend in a floral crown, jokingly designated as flower girl because everyone finds it fun. It's not like you're a paragon of tradition."

"Indeed I am. I will be in full Scots dress."

Michael sought out any excuse to wear his kilt, which wasn't surprising, since he looked so good in it. And when he said full dress, he meant it, completing the bright red-and-green Adair tartan kilt with a silver-buttoned, deep-green velvet Prince Charlie jacket and waistcoat, white tuxedo shirt with black tie, and even a *skean dhu* in the top of his hose.

"And you'll look delicious." I patted his arm. "This ceremony is all about joy and fun and celebrating our friends and their love. Now loosen up and enjoy it."

"Can't she just call you a supporter, like British men do with their friends?"

"Oh, that's so much better. It sounds like a foundation garment."

"A what?"

"Foundation garment. What we used to call bras and girdles and such. Usually implies something orthopedic and definitely not sexy."

"So nothing you'd wear." Grin.

"Nice."

"Not nice at all." He reached for me. "If I didn't have to get to plea negotiations…"

"I'd still have to get Daniel to drop-off."

"Well, there's that."

"Keep a good thought."

"Bad ones are more fun."

"Ma! Scotchie's trying to drink my milk!"

Back to work.

CHAPTER EIGHT
TRAFFIC CIRCLE THE WAGONS

The school run is the great equalizer. No matter who you are—or think you are—you have to get those kids fed, packed up, and dropped off on time. Or else. And everyone in that line is just as much a mess as you are. Whether they admit it or not.

Wednesday morning, we were all more than willing to admit it.

After what we'd seen the previous day, Corinna, Brian, and I were all looking pretty rough at drop-off. None of us had taken Old Man Loquat's suggestion for Scotch and sleep, but considering the results of our own remedies, maybe we should have.

Corinna was clutching a travel mug like it was a talisman for a good day—and who knew, maybe it was. Brian's glasses were half-tilted like he'd been rubbing his eyes and hadn't bothered to put them back down.

Me? I'd seen my pasty face and deep purple undereye circles

and thought about throwing on a little makeup or something…
and completely forgot until Corinna glanced at me and winced.

"That bad?" I asked.

"Oh, yeah." She nodded to Brian.

"Go straight home and fix up," he agreed. "You can't let anyone see you like that."

"Sorry."

"No judging," Corinna said. "That's why you have friends."

"True." Brian shuffled from foot to foot and suddenly looked down. "Oh, good Lord."

We turned to him in alarm, as he started laughing.

"What?"

"What?"

He pointed to his feet.

We burst into laughter too.

He was wearing different shoes. Well, the same dark lace-ups, just one brown, one black.

This, of course, was the precise moment Kryssie sailed into view, perfectly pulled together and all puffed up with importance, carefully cultivating a very serious face.

"What is *wrong* with you people?" she asked in a waspish tone. "We just witnessed a gruesome death yesterday and now you're laughing? Try for some decorum, for heaven's sake."

The three of us stopped laughing and met her horrified gaze with annoyance.

"Everybody handles trauma differently," said Corinna.

"Many people rely on dark humor as a coping mechanism," I added in my best lawyer voice.

"We need goofy at a time like this." Brian's comment had a steely undertone. And not for nothing: He'd earned it, considering his devastating loss.

"Well! I hope you'll do better at the PTA meeting after school."

"The what?"

Our responses were staggered a little, so it sounded like an echo: *wha-wha-wha?*

"Well, after that disaster yesterday, we clearly need an emergency PTA meeting to process and determine how to handle this. Right after school in the library. The eighth-grade school service club will keep the kids busy in the gym. Lani Wilcox's son volunteered."

I bet he did.

Lani Wilcox was Kryssie's opposite number at the middle school up the street. But Lani seemed to be much more concerned about helicoptering her son to the Ivy League than one-upping the other moms. Unless it might impinge on her main goal, in which case everyone in her path was toast. I suspected Lani had volunteered her son because there was probably some way to sell it as a leadership activity on his college applications.

"Anyhow, I'll expect to see you all at the school library this afternoon."

We mumbled assurances.

"And try to put on some lipstick, Grace...and maybe fix your shoes, Brian." With those parting shots, she swept away, having thoroughly ruined our day.

For a moment, we just stared in horrified silence.

"I suppose it's too much to hope I'll have a stroke before this afternoon," Corinna said.

"Maybe a meteor will hit my car," I said.

"If I kill myself now, I might be able to avoid the meeting *and* the end of the month tax report..." Brian said.

"You don't get out that easy, buddy," I replied. "And besides, Zooey and Pete wouldn't like it."

"Bring Pete to the PTA," Corinna said. "Make Kryssie wonder. And pretzel herself trying to seem open-minded."

"Y'know," Brian said, a wicked gleam in his eye, "Pete might just enjoy that."

"Don't poke the bear," I warned. "Everything's fun until Kryssie comes up with some new boneheaded idea."

"She's right," Corinna said. "If you're not careful, you'll end up in charge of the school's Pride Day celebration or something."

"Yeah...no." Brian shook his head. "I've got enough on my plate as it is."

"No kidding," I said. "I don't know if I can even get there."

"We have been summoned, gang, and you'd better get

there." Corinna scowled at us. "You aren't going to leave me alone with that mess."

"Oh, fine." I sighed. "I'm home finishing an editing project today. Want me to bring the coffee?"

"You are an angel," pronounced Brian.

No, I thought, *I just work for one.*

"Okay, so I'll be there with three triple Americanos from Louisa's."

"That just might do it." Corinna smiled and pulled her keys out of the pocket of her long spice-red puffer. "Give us something to look forward to."

Ten minutes later, I was back at the house, enjoying a love attack from Scotchie when my phone rang. Unfamiliar number with no spam flag.

Only one person that could be.

"Grace Adair," I said in my best professional tone, thanking my lucky stars my caller couldn't see what a mess I was.

"Well, good to hear you sounding like a decently employed adult, Grace."

The crystalline enunciation with just a tiny trace of swing told me I'd guessed right.

Professor Sally Munroe, my law school mentor and the Mother who'd chosen me to join the sisterhood, would never allow herself anything as inelegant as an accent, but her voice still carried an echo of the rhythm of her Southern youth—if, and only if, you knew to listen for it.

"Thank you, Professor," I replied, taking my medicine like a good little girl. She'd upbraided me for answering my phone with a simple hello after I'd returned to court work—and she was right.

Those the professor loves, she corrects.

"How is your family? Husband and son well, and giant dog cheerful as ever?"

"Yes. How was your husband's birthday in Cancún?"

"Delightful. We may have to spend the holidays there every year." Small wicked chuckle. "There is something especially festive about welcoming the New Year in a hot tub on the beach."

"Oh, my," I said. "I could definitely go for that."

"It was delicious," agreed the professor, who was probably well into her seventies—and had just celebrated her husband's fiftieth in Mexico.

For a moment, we were both silent at the happy thought of a warm holiday night.

And then chilly reality returned.

"Margaret tells me her fiancé has had a scrape," the professor said, her tone now calm and clinical, with no trace of the Southern swing.

"He has. He and a prosecutor friend were arrested for following a man they put away years ago in a nasty bullying attack on a young girl."

"Cathie Holman, Margaret said."

"Yes."

"I'm not familiar with all of the details, but I understand it was a brutal gang assault, both physically and emotionally."

"That's correct."

"Not sexually, though."

"Not explicitly, no. But the whole thing was triggered by Cathie's drawing the notice of a Mean Girl's boyfriend, so there was a strong undertone of sexual humiliation. Or at least an intent to render her permanently unappealing."

"Vile." The professor encapsulated an entire universe of disapproval in the single, lingering syllable.

"Vile indeed," I agreed. "And since the victim lived, and the attackers were young…and probably also because there was no sexual assault, most were treated as first-time offenders or juveniles—and none drew the sentence they truly deserved."

"Ah." A pause as the professor considered the situation. "So is Al planning some kind of direct vengeance, or just hoping to catch this man in another offense?"

"I believe the latter." At least I could say that with confidence. "He and his prosecutor friend—a mentor of mine—are both extremely ethical, and highly unlikely to play vigilante."

"Well, that is encouraging, at least."

I waited. There was more.

"But the whole matter is extremely troubling. It raises serious questions about Al and what kind of spouse he would be to Margaret."

I noted the "would" where a "will" should be and offered a non-committal "Uh-huh."

"I'm not certain the Mothers can countenance a match with a man who appears to be a loose cannon."

"With respect, professor, I think that's a bit overstated. He and my prosecutor friend are keeping tabs on one man from one case. They've never taken direct action, and—I suspect, but can't prove—would probably not have been arrested if an overzealous young officer was not trying to make a point."

"All of that is true, Grace. And I do trust your judgment, as you know. There are enough mitigating factors here that I don't think it's appropriate to simply stop the marriage."

"No."

"But that's still very much on the table if we don't get satisfactory assurances that Al and his friend will not pursue this. I've explained this to Margaret, and she understands everything at stake."

"I understand too." I also understood I'd be getting a panicky call from Madge very soon.

"I'm sure you do." She took a breath, let it out in a sigh. "You have a gift for finding a way forward in the most impossible situations. Do you think there's one here?"

"I do, actually." I wasn't lying. Might have been overly optimistic, though. "If I find a way to get iron-clad assurances from Al and Vince that they will no longer pursue this, will that be satisfactory to the Mothers?"

"Do you have something in mind?"

"I don't have a complete plan," I admitted. "But I have a good sense of what might convince them to be compliant—without, of course, giving away Madge's secrets—and I may be able to come up with something."

"I'm not sure I like the sound of that, Grace. We don't traffic in blackmail or extortion."

"No, no, professor," I said quickly. "What I meant is, they're both stand-up guys, and if I find the right appeal to their sense of honor, perhaps I can convince them to make some sort of vow..."

"A vow to forswear vengeance? Hmm." Professor Munroe tapped a fingernail on her phone.

"These are men of their word."

"I'm aware. So, yes, if you can find a way to convince them to make a sacred vow to drop this matter, it will be sufficient."

"Thank you."

"But if not..."

She didn't need to complete the sentence.

"I understand."

CHAPTER NINE
WE NEED TO TALK

D espite the rocky start, I got a good bit of work done on my editing project and managed to score a badly needed nap before fixing myself up for the afternoon. Corinna was right. There was no way I could run around looking like that, especially considering we'd be dealing with Kryssie at her most officious.

So, while I had the confidence supplied by good concealer, a flick of mascara, and a dab of bright pink lip balm, I was still feeling more than slightly mutinous when I pulled into the Rowland parking lot that afternoon.

Fair to say no one else was in a sunshiny mood as we straggled in for the big PTA sit-down. My pals were waiting on the sidewalk when I walked up. I held out the cardboard tray from Louisa's, and each silently took their triple Americano with a grateful sigh.

On the way into the hall, we compared notes.

Corinna had spent the day trying to find a way to reconcile the book club's requests with the latest numbers from the town council and a budget gap that looked more like a chasm. Brian and Old Man Loquat were trying to track down heirloom tomato seeds for spring, because their usual company had lost their harvest in a brush fire. And you know how my day was going.

"Y'know," Corinna said, patting Brian's arm, "you're the one who really needs some trauma help. You three were so close to it."

"Yeah," I agreed. "Are you doing okay?"

"We really didn't see anything," Brian said. I wasn't sure if the wince was a sign of trouble or just a reaction to a painful memory.

But it sure didn't ease my concerns.

I caught a glimpse of the three of us in the glass door as we walked in. Even neatened up, we were pretty much a mess.

Fortunately, Kryssie was perky enough for all of us.

Inside the library, she was in her element, wearing a carefully concerned face, but—in a dead giveaway—prettied up in a long beige knit dress and cardigan set I was sure cost more than my wedding band, hair freshly blown out for the occasion. Her mane swished as she flitted from the principal to the counselor to the school resource officer. The principal and counselor had to maintain a professional game face, but the resource officer, a former colleague of Al's who was picking up a little work to help with the grandkids' college fund, couldn't stop an eye roll.

We were right with her.

The three of us sat in an unobtrusive corner near the back. Brian, who had the best spatial-relations skills, noted that the door behind us opened right into the corridor near the gym, where the kids were enjoying whatever activities Lani Wilcox's son had concocted. We were close enough to hear the noise filtering out, and we exchanged smiles.

Lani Wilcox's son was going to earn that line on his college application.

And we were going to earn our parenting credentials too, I suspected.

"All right, people!" Kryssie clapped, an amazingly loud sound in the library, which was supposed to be for whispers and quiet intellectual discussion.

Okay, maybe not intellectual discussion among elementary schoolers, but you get the idea.

"Why don't we open with a moment of silence for our poor dear victim. A terrible loss to education and the world, and such a nice man, Eric...Egan."

Subtle eye rolls ping-ponging between the three of us. They looked like I felt: unsure whether to retch at the irony of this guy being called a nice man—or chuckle at Kryssie's near-forgetting of his name.

Of course, this wasn't about him.

Probably just as well.

No, this moment was all about Kryssie.

A subtle toss of her hair as she continued. "Now, we're here today to talk about how we can help our children, who were so traumatized by yesterday's incident. We need to get them as much support as we can, and surround them with all the..."

Kryssie went on for a while in that vein, warming to the topic of what our poor, traumatized children might need. As she droned on, the counselor and school resource officer's expressions went from bored to annoyed, to very nearly alarmed.

When Kryssie started talking about holding regular discussion sessions to process the trauma, we looked up, unable to conceal our own alarm.

It also drew a nudge and a glance from the counselor, which got the principal to step in.

"Well, thank you so much, Kryssie. Let's turn this over to Dr. Garrity for some constructive strategies for helping our kids handle this."

Dr. Garrity, a fortyish woman with kind eyes I recognized from the Friends of the Library, offered some actual common-sense advice, much more in the mold of Old Man Loquat's thoughts on talking it through and moving on than Kryssie's overwrought nattering about our poor traumatized kids.

As the meeting wound down, the three of us started for our

secret escape and almost walked into another savvy sneak: JakesPop.

"You know about this shortcut too?" Brian asked him.

"Yup." He nodded and opened the door.

The four of us walked into the hall, and I hung back with JakesPop.

"How's Jake holding up?" I asked.

The man winced.

"Oh, I'm sorry."

"He's fine," he said quickly. "It was just a tough day."

"That it was," I agreed. "Did you see it happen?"

"Um," he mumbled.

"You and Jake were in the group on the train, right?"

"Yeah." His eyes focused sharply on me for a moment.

Then howls from the gym.

"Gotta go," he said.

"Yeah—take care."

"You too."

Much later, I would wonder if there was something strange in his tone—and if it would have made a difference if I'd heard it.

At that point, though, the only thing that mattered was getting our kids out of the madness in the gym. Brian was first to the door, and threw it open to reveal a scene straight from some bad sitcom:

A tall, lanky tween I assumed was Lani Wilcox's son was cowering against the back wall under the basketball hoop, as kids threw red balls at him, chanting, "Dodgeball, dodgeball!"

There were, however, so many kids and so many balls that there was no point in trying to dodge, so he'd clearly given up and decided to wait out the onslaught.

"STOP!" Corinna yelled, with all the authority of a librarian who's spent her adult life shushing people.

The remaining balls dropped from small hands.

"All right, you little maniacs," she snapped, "get those balls back into the hamper—now."

The maniacs, who included Jake, but thankfully none of our own cherubs, meekly started scooping up the balls.

The big kid unfolded himself and came over to Corinna. "ImanisMom! Thank you so much," he babbled. "It was like *Lord of the Flies*. I didn't know the little ones—"

"They're scarier than you think," I assured him, as Brian and I walked over to our kids, who were in a small knot giggling with Cherise.

They looked up.

"You're better than this," Brian said.

"What he said," I added. "Just because you didn't throw anything doesn't mean you did the right thing."

"But—" the kids started, slightly staggered as if in a round.

Brian glared. "I don't expect you to jump in front of the firing squad, but it would be awfully nice if you'd try to get help for the poor guy."

"At the very least," I said, "you didn't have to egg them on."

"Cherise Ruby Grant," Corinna pronounced as she walked over to us. "Were you involved in this shameful display?"

"No, Mama."

"Good answer. Come along. You can apologize to Jason on the way out."

"As can you," I said to Daniel.

"And you," Brian to Zooey.

The next few minutes were not especially comfortable for either parents or children. But once Daniel and I were settled in the car and heading for home, I waited for a stoplight and caught his eye in the rearview mirror.

"Hey, buddy."

"Yes, Ma?"

"Good job at the end there."

His eyes widened behind the glasses, making him look even more like a baby owl than usual. "Good?"

"Yeah, sweetheart. You made a mistake, and you apologized and made it right. That's what decent people do."

"Oh."

"Nobody's perfect, honey. Everybody does dumb things. Sometimes dumb, hurtful things. But you learn from them and do better next time."

"Better next time?"

"Yeah. It's like Zooey's dad said. Nobody expects you to put yourself in danger to stop something, but you can always run off to get help."

"I can, can't I?"

"Yep. Getting help is being a hero too."

"Okay, Ma, we'll be heroes next time."

He said it like a vow. Like the kind of vow I was going to be demanding of Vince and Al very soon.

I suspected I was going to have a lot more luck with my little guy.

A couple of turns later, I pulled into our driveway just as my phone buzzed.

I laughed when I saw the post in the group chat, from Corinna:

"Nice teachable moment. PARENTING WIN."

I added my thumbs-up and heart emojis to Brian's.

Take the victories where you can.

CHAPTER TEN
MEANWHILE, BACK AT THE RANCH

"You look like I feel," Michael said as he walked into the kitchen that evening, skillfully balancing plates and silverware. "I thought today was a home day."

"PTA meeting after school about the aquarium mess. Wanted to make sure we're 'protecting the children.'"

"Ah."

"Let's just say they have a much different idea of how to handle it than we do. Old Man Loquat is right—you need to acknowledge it and then take the kids' leads. The PTA chair wanted to bring in counselors and have daily sharing sessions and—"

"No." Michael's voice was calm, and definite. "We're not doing that to our kid."

"Damn right we're not. Fortunately, the counselor wasn't into it."

"Dr. Garrity? Smart lady."

"Yep. She, at least, gets it." I nodded. "We should check in once in a while, but he is not going to define himself as one of the kids who was there when something bad happened."

"Exactly." Michael set the plates in the sink and started rinsing.

The plate carrying was just his usual helpful spouse routine. The rinsing suggested something else.

I met his gaze. "So?"

"So you had a tough day."

"And?"

Sheepish grin. "Damn that Celtic radar of yours."

"Nothing ethnic about it." I stepped in and started pulling plates from the sink to load into the dishwasher. "Just been married to you for a while, partner."

"Well, there's that." He watched as I finished loading the plates and silverware. As I straightened up, I noticed his appreciative expression.

Nothing wrong with a spouse who still thinks you're hot. Especially when he's pretty cute himself.

"Give it up, pal," I said as I closed the machine.

He came up behind me and put his hands on my shoulders, rubbing the tight muscles at the base of my neck. This must be some ask.

"How would you like to work on something that is as far from the PTA as it's possible to be tomorrow?"

I leaned back to meet his gaze. "How bad is it?"

"Not bad at all."

I narrowed my eyes.

"Honest." He stopped massaging and rested his chin on my shoulder. "Need you to take an arraignment in a really sad case."

"How sad?"

"She's nineteen. Got arrested trying to steal a handful of bracelets at a boutique on the Green. Fought the officers, had drugs on her. Spending the night in the lockup and the family is looking into rehab clinics for her."

"Not a poor family, then?"

"No." He sighed. "Not stupid rich, but well-off enough to give her a good start. Which seemed to be what was happening until a really bad sports injury a year ago."

"I thought the docs had gotten smarter about giving pain-killers to kids."

"When they put a titanium rod in your leg, they have to give you something pretty strong."

"True enough." I folded my arms and turned back to him, leaning on the sink. "So we're going to try to move this to drug court and get her some help?"

"Yep."

"Trying to save another stray, huh?"

Rueful smile from Michael. "It's not pro bono."

"I didn't say it was." Not that he hadn't helped his share over the years. "And?"

"It may not be an easy lift. The police report says she tried to bite a cop."

"Tried?"

"The only reason we have a shot is that she didn't succeed. History of violence is a deal-breaker."

"Right."

"We're going to have to convince the judge that Lis—that's the girl's name—was just flailing around in terror and isn't a real threat to anyone."

"No previous record?"

"Nope."

"Sports injury…big, strong girl?"

"Nope. Tiny little thing. Described as a spark plug when she was playing lacrosse…now rail thin."

I nodded. "What about attitude? Privilege?"

He shook his head. "Definitely not the privileged princess type. When I saw her, she was curled up in a corner of the holding cell. Parents seem anguished and low-key. I don't think we have to worry about her rubbing anyone the wrong way."

"Good." There was still something he wasn't telling me. "Who's doing arraignments tomorrow?"

A slight wince told me I'd hit the mark. "Weird quirk in the schedule. It's Burdette."

"The Judge Burdette?" As in Veronica Burns Burdette, the jurist who'd almost sent him to jail for contempt when he got a little too zealous in the defense of an earlier client. I'd come in, talked him down, and smoothed things over with Judge Burdette, who knew and liked me from my prosecuting days.

Well, that explained everything.

"Yes. This kid shouldn't suffer just because I don't get along with the judge."

"Hello, Captain Understatement."

Michael narrowed those sparkly green-gold eyes at me. "So?"

"So arraignments start early, and Judge Burdette doesn't mess around. If you can drop off Daniel, I'll take it."

"Deal. I'll even make him breakfast, so you don't have to rush getting dressed."

"Wow."

"Survey on the news said women find their men sexier when they do their part in the house."

I laughed. "It would be impossible to find you sexier. Well, except in your kilt, of course."

"That reminds me, can you drop my shirt at the cleaners tomorrow? Everything else is fine, since I just had it pressed for the Robert Burns dinner."

Michael and I go to Robert Burns's birthday celebration every January at the home of one of his legal pals, involving full Scots attire and a fair amount of Scotch. It's essentially a celebration of Scottish heritage and culture, conveniently marking the birthday of Scotland's most beloved bard. Unlike many of these affairs, though, it's not especially athletic. Michael's friends don't dance the reels. They read poetry and tell stories, which means little wear and tear on the full-dress outfit.

"Sure," I said. "The cleaner's on the way home."

"Dad! Scotchie wants to play!"

Michael gave me a quick kiss. "Gotta go for dad time."

I grinned. "That's pretty appealing too."

CHAPTER ELEVEN
THE CLIENT

"Good luck with this one." Bailiff Pearl Edwards gave me a wry little eye roll as she opened the door to the client consultation room. "Apparently tried to bite one of the arresting officers yesterday."

"Still violent?" I asked.

"Nah. Wet noodle now...and she's a tiny little thing anyhow." Edwards shrugged. "At this point, she's not dangerous, just sad. Not engaging much."

"Might be better that way." I didn't mind at all if my client stayed out of the way and let me do my thing. Especially if she'd been violent earlier. The bite was probably going to be a problem.

"Hello, Miss Allen?" I asked as I stepped inside, using the cool professional voice to set the tone.

A small pile of gray rags at the table stirred, revealing a girl about the size of a middle-schooler, with burning eyes just visible from a tangle of dark hair.

"You…" she started in a rusty whisper.

"I'm Grace Adair, your attorney," I said. "I'll be defending you at arraignment, and we'll try to get the case transferred to drug court."

The eyes flickered. Fear. She reminded me of nothing so much as a cornered animal. Probably tried to bite the officer in a fight-or-flight reflex. I could work with this. And certainly, her small size would make her seem less dangerous.

Moving slowly and carefully, as I would with a frightened child or animal, I sat opposite her at the table. She watched my every move, flinching momentarily when my brief bag ended up a little too close to her as I set it down.

"What…" she started. "What happens now?"

"Well, hopefully, you get help."

"Help?"

Somewhere in the depths of those wretched eyes stirred a tiny spark.

Hope?

"Yes. Your family has already found you a rehab program and submitted the paperwork to the court. I'm going to show all of this to the judge and ask her to transfer the case to drug court."

"Okay…"

"If that happens, the focus will be on help, not punishment, and with any luck, you'll get the space to get better."

"Better." She took a breath and pushed her hair back, show-ing bony white hands, and revealing a heart-shaped face that might have been beautiful when she was sober and healthy.

"Better." I gave her a friendly but businesslike smile. "But you need to do your part now."

"What's that?"

"Pretty much what you're doing now. Be calm, quiet—and please don't bite the bailiff."

"This big guy picked me up and dragged me away—I was scared." Her voice was fast and breathy, and I didn't doubt she'd been terrified. Unfortunately, everyone involved in the case now knew she tended to fight and bite when frightened.

Not ideal when I was trying to present her as a non-violent offender.

Still, we had a pretty good shot because the judge had been involved in the creation of the drug courts. And I'd worked well with her during my time as a prosecutor.

Edwards knocked on the door.

"All right, Miss Allen," I said, "let's go."

Lis Allen gave me a stunned glance. "You're calling me Miss, like I'm a person."

"You *are* a person, Miss Allen." I smiled. "Whatever you've done, whatever evil has you in its grip, you are still a human created in the image of God, and you deserve basic respect."

"Oh." She rose and stood shakily for an instant, holding on to the table.

"You can do this."

She bit her chapped lower lip, giving me a glimpse of straight white teeth, suggesting she'd taken good care of herself—or been well-cared for—before all of this. "All right."

Inside the courtroom, Judge Veronica Burns Burdette was finishing another routine arraignment, and it looked like there was one more to go before us. Lis watched that hearing with frightened intensity, her eyes widening when the judge glared at the public defender and told him his assault defendant had better stay out of sports bars, no matter which team was playing.

Kind of a problem with the big game coming up.

I suspected the guy would be back here before Valentine's Day to get a high bail—but that wasn't my responsibility.

"All right, what's next?"

Edwards intoned: "Elizabeth Marie Allen, birthdate September 22, 2005, shoplifting, drug possession, disorderly conduct, resisting arrest."

Born within a few weeks of the Cathie Holman attack. Suddenly, I felt amazingly old.

"So, Mr. Dix?" she turned to the assistant state's attorney, the same guy I'd dealt with on a recent murder case. He had been very young and pretty clueless then, and I had no reason to assume he'd improved.

I was not displeased.

"Well, Your Honor, the defendant grabbed a handful of jewelry from a display at the Butterfly Boutique and tried to leave. The clerk stopped her, and when a New Haven officer arrived to investigate, she struggled with him and tried to bite him. A search revealed drugs on her person."

My client tensed, like she wanted to argue. I patted her shoulder and was surprised at how bony she was under the grubby, oversized hoodie.

"Did she actually bite the officer?" asked Judge Burdette.

"No, ma'am." Dix looked disappointed. "The officer was unharmed."

Judge Burdette turned her focus to me. "Ms. MacInnes Adair?"

"Thank you, Your Honor." I nodded to Lis. "My client does not contest the substance of the allegations. But we believe she is an excellent candidate for the state's special drug courts."

"Is she, now?" Judge Burdette leaned forward. Dix couldn't stop an irritated sigh, drawing a glare from the judge.

"Yes, Your Honor. She has no previous criminal record and no history of violence. What she does have is an all-too-common misfortune." As I launched into the argument, I silently thanked our paralegal Annie for her excellent case history. "Until a year and a half ago, she was a straight-A student, happy, healthy, and planning for a future that certainly did not include stealing costume jewelry and struggling with police officers. Then she sustained a compound fracture in a lacrosse game. While doctors have become much more cautious with painkillers in general, the deep pain from a major orthopedic injury still often requires opioids with all their attendant risks. Despite good care and strong family support, my client was one of the unlucky ones who could not stave off addiction."

"Ah." The judge was riding with me.

"She—and her family—are taking this situation as a bright-line call for an intervention. They've secured her a bed at a good rehab facility and are prepared to make sure she follows the program."

Judge Burdette looked through the paperwork I indicated. Lis was sitting at the table, hands folded, chin resting on them, with that frightened-animal stare again.

"You say she has no history of violence?" the judge asked.

"What about the biting?" Dix cut in.

Judge Burdette shot him a glance. "I was just about to ask, Dix. You might want to wait until it's your turn to speak."

"With respect to Your Honor and my learned colleague, there was no actual biting. She had a fight-or-flight reaction, quite possibly intensified by whatever substances were in her body at the time. And even then, she didn't attack anyone. She simply struggled to protect herself."

"Hm." The judge looked at Lis. "What do you have to say for yourself, young lady?"

"Um, I—I need help."

Judge Burdette nodded. "I tend to agree. Case transferred to drug court. Defendant ROR with the condition that she report to rehab today."

Released on her own recognizance and off to rehab. Best possible outcome.

"Your Honor—" Dix offered a protest even he had to know was pointless.

"Save your fire for when it works, Dix," the judge replied crisply.

"Thank you, Your Honor," I said.

"Your client is a textbook case for the drug courts, counselor. I'd be remiss in not sending her there."

"Again, thank you."

"Always a pleasure, Ms. MacInnes Adair."

This time, her use of my name registered, and I thought: *Ooh, I like that.* I don't hyphenate, but I do use all three names for formal matters. Maybe that's how I should bill myself from here on.

I noodled about it for the next hour or so as we went through the formalities, and I turned my client over to her parents, a prosperous but very stressed-looking pair who actually seemed interested and involved.

As I walked out, I figured this one would be off the radar for a while. Hopefully for good.

Dix was in the lobby, drinking a coffee from the cart, and he alerted when he saw me. "You got a minute?"

"If it's really just a minute. I've got a slew of things to do before school pickup." And one of those things was get back to the house and change into mom clothes. I wasn't going to let this mope keep me from being comfortable for the rest of my busy day.

"Do you have any idea what's going on with Mr. Scupper?"

"I'm sorry?"

"You're the closest I can get. I know his daughter exists, but I have no idea where she is or how to find her."

"You wouldn't. He keeps family and work rigorously separate."

"Right. I know." Adam Dix blushed. "He keeps telling me to find and marry some nice young person—that's how he puts it because he wants to be open-minded—so I'm not alone."

"Well, he's probably right," I said. "If it's the nice young person you belong with."

"Like the One?"

"Exactly like the One." I patted his arm. "Vince—like everyone who's been blessed with a good marriage—is a fan of the institution. Even if he's widowed."

"Loss is the price of love."

"Attributed to Queen Elizabeth, and a very good insight." I nodded. "But you didn't seek me out to get my thoughts on marriage."

"No, even though they're very helpful, ma'am."

Ma'am? I might have to kill this puppy. Kidding. Probably. "Oh?"

"Mr. Scupper is acting weird. Distracted. At least since last month. I'm afraid he might be sick."

"Any sign of illness?"

"No. It's just the way he's acting...I don't know any other

way to explain it. Reminds me of how my grandpa was just before we found out he'd run out of treatments."

It was, of course, possible that Vince had some kind of terrible illness. It was far more likely that his distraction stemmed from his efforts to observe Ethan Storey and the resulting trouble. How to calm down the puppy without giving Vince away?

I patted his arm. "Look, I'm glad you asked me. I can't tell you why it's happening, but I know he's a little wound over Al's wedding. Might be as simple as it reminds him of his own loss."

Dix's pasty face went red, and his eyes widened. "Oh, crap. I should have thought of that."

"He misses Marie terribly," I said with perfect truth, "and big events like this bring up memories. That's not always a good thing."

"Jeez. What can I do—"

"Absolutely nothing, Dix." I made very direct eye contact. "Old-school guys like Vince don't want to admit they have feelings, never mind that those feelings are obvious to anyone else."

"Oh."

"The best thing you can possibly do for Vince is just keep a really close eye on the work stuff. Make sure he doesn't miss anything that could bite him later."

"I think I can do that."

I'd seen him in court. Somewhere under all that messy dirty-blond hair was a half-decent legal mind. "I know you can. Be his backstop. And make sure he never sees it."

His eyes widened a bit as he absorbed the idea of supporting his mentor. It's a moment in anyone's career, when you realize that you sometimes have to help the people you look up to. "Okay."

A church clock started chiming. Eleven o'clock.

I patted Dix's arm one more time. "You got this…and I gotta get moving."

"Thanks, Ms. Adair."

"Don't mention it. Please."

CHAPTER TWELVE
NOT SO LUCKY LUCIANO

As I pulled out of Michael's parking lot, my phone buzzed. Unfamiliar number with a New Haven area code. Not Professor Munroe, whose burners never had a recognizable exchange.

"Grace Adair."

"Hi, Grace. It's Carla Luciano."

Lieutenant Carla Luciano, of course. The fact that she didn't use the title meant we were off the record. Probably.

"Hi, Carla. How are you?"

"I'd be better if my twelve-year-old hadn't just announced that her science project is due Friday—as in tomorrow."

"The project you didn't know about until just now?"

"That's the one." Dry little laugh. "And before I head off to the craft store, I need some background on the aquarium death."

"Ah. And since I was chaperoning…"

"…and you're a trained observer, not to mention an officer of the court, I thought you might be able to give me a bit of background info."

"I can do that." I looked at the dashboard clock. Amazingly, only eleven-thirty. "I've got a couple hours before pickup time."

"How much would you hate meeting me at Craft World?"

"Considering I need a few things too, I wouldn't hate it at all. Twenty minutes?"

"See you there."

In the middle of the day on a Thursday in late January, the only people at Craft World were grandmas and harried parents on their lunch hours. Carla Luciano was at the Valentine's Day seasonal display at the door when I walked in.

"Thinking ahead?" I asked.

"Actually, feeling kind of nostalgic. She's reached the stage where valentines are icky."

I smiled. "It is kind of fun destroying the dining room table to put it all together."

"Yeah." Rueful shrug. "Can't imagine why I miss it. Took me a month to get the glitter out of my hair the last time. Except I didn't know it was the last time."

"That's the problem with kids. For every first there's a last." I looked at the packets of red and pink glitter pens. "Some days I miss the baby and toddler stage."

"Yeah," Carla said with the wistful note in her voice competing with a dry eyebrow flick.

"And then I think I need my head examined."

Shared chuckle.

"Isn't that the truth." She took one more look at the hearts and flowers and shook it off. "I need to find some posterboard and stick-on letters. They're studying the elements, and Sofia is in charge of the noble gases."

"Nice. I didn't realize they started chemistry so early."

"New pilot program. School's trying out a special accelerated curriculum."

"Curriculum?" My radar perked up at the mention, and my new friend, who is, after all, still a cop, caught it immediately.

"That's right," she said. "The late Mr. Egan was a curriculum guy."

"Elementary curriculum," I added as we started walking toward the posterboard aisle.

"He worked for a private company and apparently had a teaching degree but no certification."

"I knew about the degree," I said, debating how much to give away. Carla Luciano would be an extremely valuable source on both of my current issues, and I could drop a few things without giving any real indication of where I'd gotten them. Front a little bit of info and get more, maybe. "I'm pretty sure he went to a religious seminary. He made an offhand mention of being a former priest once...and very quickly changed the subject."

"As anyone would these days." Carla nodded. "He was at a New Jersey parish, a junior pastor under a predatory priest. He left early in the criminal case."

"Not charged, right?"

"No. But as you know, that doesn't mean he was innocent. Only that they couldn't prove guilt."

"Right. And with something like this..."

"Precisely."

We had reached the presentation supplies aisle, which was loaded with every color, thickness, and configuration of posterboard and backgrounds. Overwhelming as always.

"Sofia wants vapor blue for the noble gases," Carla said, moving to a display of boards. "Do you think this works?"

"It's a good color," I agreed, taking a close look at the soft blue, "but do you need a flat board or the three-panel display?"

"Thankfully, we're doing a flat board this time. They'll put them together with the other elements."

"Whew. Those three-panel numbers are a nightmare. Daniel did one on polar bears last fall, and I thought we'd never get it filled."

"Oh, yeah." Carla pulled out the board and looked at it. "This will definitely work."

I nodded. "Pretty color. When I was a kid, they only had the primary colors."

"Right? So much better now." She nodded to the end of the aisle. "What do you need?"

"Some of those nice cheap markers—we're always running

dry—and glue for sure. He's doing a collage about the dog."

"Fun."

"It actually is—they're learning about adjectives in language arts, so he's doing words about Scotchie. 'Fuzzy,' 'blond,' 'loyal.'"

"Nice." As we walked, she returned to the topic at hand. "So it was a known thing that Egan was a former priest?"

"I think some people knew, but it wasn't something he broadcast. When he mentioned it to me, it was a slip."

"But if you knew…"

"Other parents would know too. Exactly."

"And seeing him with kids might trigger something."

"Sure could. There are an awful lot of folks out there who have reason to be triggered by the idea of a former priest near their kid." I shook my head.

"True." She pointed to the next aisle. "I think that's where the glue is."

"Thanks."

"Tell me about the train," she said. "It looked pretty secure."

"Seemed that way to me too. My group rode it first. The cars seemed sturdy enough, and everyone was supposed to be wearing seatbelts." I took a breath. "A couple folks I know who were on the tram say they didn't see anything. Just that they looked up and heard the grunt and crash."

Pretty much verbatim what Brian and Pete had said while we were all milling around getting on the buses. And all I had. Of course, I didn't share my misgivings about the guys, hoping they'd never go beyond vague concerns.

Carla nodded. "That's what the witness statements say. I'm still lining up where everybody was, but it all seemed to happen fast."

"Yes," I agreed. "My group was down with the baby beluga, and we didn't have any warning."

"So somebody just came up to him and shoved him over the car wall."

"Not an easy task."

"No. Be interesting to see the toxicology report, I think."

"I think you may be right on that. Could be a lot easier to

throw him over if he were impaired." I thought about it. "That day, he seemed a bit tired, but not actively impaired. But I wasn't in his group, so I would not have seen him right before it happened."

"One more thing for the re-interviews." She nodded and pointed. "Do you want regular glue sticks, purple, or glitter?"

"Oh, glitter. It's still a thing."

"Even for boys?"

"Absolutely. The first-grade definition of masculinity is not threatened by glitter." I tossed a couple glittery glue sticks in my basket.

"Threatened masculinity," Carla said. "Be good to know if anyone on that train had a run-in with a predator priest."

"It would," I agreed. And bad to let her know about the vibe I'd gotten from Pete. "You'll probably want to check the settlement records."

"Settlements?"

"Well, you know the Church has made some massive payouts for abuse in recent years," I explained. "Sometimes there are records of specific payments. Not always—depending on the court and the process, names can be redacted. Amounts almost always are. You can also backtrack it by hometown and parish."

"Sounds like a research nightmare."

"It could be. Probably something more for the state's attorney at trial." I shrugged. "But it's a way to prove motive."

"Which could help." She took a breath. Thought for a moment. "I need to get some stick-on letters. I think that's the next aisle."

"It is. I need them too."

"Thanks for this," she said as we walked. "You've been a big help."

"Glad to. I don't think anybody's in favor of people getting murdered in front of kids."

"Amen to that." She reached for two packets of letters. "Metallic or black?"

"Oh, absolutely metallic. They're elements after all."

Carla grinned. "Y'know, we should do this more often."

"I agree."

"Will you be at Al and Madge's wedding?"

"I'm the flower girl."

"Um, okay…" Slight double take.

"See, Al's daughter is Madge's matron of honor, just as her son is his best man. But we're really close and she wanted me to have a role."

"And you've always wanted to be a flower girl."

"Got it in one." I did a little flounce. "But seriously, it's just a treat to be in the middle of all the love and joy."

"Oh, I'm with you there. Where are they registered anyhow?"

"Feed the Kids and the Domestic Violence Resource Center."

The grin and a nod. "Yep. That's Al. He worked with them to set up a better process for dealing with survivors."

"I think I heard that somewhere. Makes sense. He's a real stand-up guy and very protective."

"But supportive," she said. "He was my mentor on the homicide squad. Told me he always thought about how he'd want his daughter treated."

"He's pretty terrific. I'm really glad he and Madge ended up together." My phone dinged. "Oh, hell."

"What?"

"Client. I'm still doing a little editing for long-standing clients and one's on deadline." The phone clock said just after noon—which would give me more than an hour to work if I got back to Alcott right now. "I have to scoot."

"So should I. Burned my lunch hour for this, but well worth it. Thanks."

"Thank you. See you at the wedding if not sooner."

"Hopefully not too much sooner."

I joined her grim nod. "Got that."

CHAPTER THIRTEEN
ENTER DON NUNZIO

In the evening, Michael arrived almost on time, carrying a floral arrangement.

"To what do I owe this?" I asked.

"Wasn't me," he replied with an embarrassed smile, handing it over.

Once I got a good look, I knew he was telling the truth. When Michael brought me flowers, it was either classic red roses on Valentine's Day or the lavender-pink ones I'd carried at our wedding. There wasn't a rose in sight here: it was a milk glass bowl filled with bright-colored gerbera daisies. It looked like something you'd send your grandma.

"What?" I asked.

"Check the card."

My jaw dropped as I read:

With appreciation, Nunzio Imperiale.

"Is that—"

"Yep." He gave me a nervous smile. "Don Nunzio is the uncle

of your new client. He wanted her sent to rehab, and he called us instead of his usual attorney because he didn't want anyone with a whiff of mob lawyer about them to take the case."

"Hence, me, the former prosecutor." I should have known there was more to it than Judge Burdette. It would have made far more sense for Michael to just mend fences with her.

"No, hence you, the Adair who was available for arraignment court that day." Michael shook his head. "I didn't get you into this deliberately. But it turns out that Don Nunzio is both pleased and impressed—and it's not a bad thing to be on his good side."

"We aren't…" I started.

"Of course not. I have zero desire to become a Mafia lawyer. But the Don is actually a pretty good guy, for a murderous mob boss, and he cares about his family. Nothing to worry about here."

"No?"

"No. This is the old-school mob. Women and children are non-combatants and off-limits. No one is going to come after me, or more importantly, you, for defending her. And the fact that I have a very smart wife who spends most of her time at home but occasionally helps a deserving client is simply something interesting for the Don to know. If anything, he probably respects you because you're a full-time mother and part-time lawyer."

"That's all?"

"That's all. It does neither of us any harm for the Don to have goodwill toward us."

"Okay…"

"Defense lawyers never know what they're going to need to know, or who might bring them useful information. So I'm not entirely displeased that we're on the Don's good side."

"And that's all it is."

"That," he said, taking the bowl from me and placing it on the speaker stand below the TV, "is precisely all it is."

"Okay, then."

"What's for dinner…don't say chicken parm."

"Chicken, green beans, and stovetop stuffing," I replied. I'd decided on that menu on the way home. It was almost as quick as my go-to chicken dish and didn't come with a fight.

"Excellent." He grinned.

The rest of the evening's drama was strictly domestic, as Michael and I helped Daniel finish the language arts project about Scotchie, and Daniel announced, as he walked off to bed, that he needed two dozen cookies for the monthly birthday celebration the next day.

Of course he did.

I bet Perry Mason never stayed up late baking cookies for first graders.

CHAPTER FOURTEEN
ONE OF *THOSE* MORNINGS

Some days you know it's over the moment you get out of bed and your feet hit the cold floor. When, for example, your heel lands on the scrunchie you took out of your ponytail last night, and you almost fall on your backside.

The universe was trying to tell me something, and I should have listened.

I would have plenty of time to reflect on that later.

Just at that moment, though, as Michael stirred slightly but didn't wake up, I wasn't into introspection. Too much to do.

On the way downstairs, I started the coffee and checked to be sure Daniel's cookies were ready. That was when I realized Daniel hadn't given me his lunch bag at the end of the day, so I was stuck cleaning all the little containers before I could pack them. Five minutes I'd have to find.

Even if I had to pay for it later, I was going to get in some kind of exercise. After I filled Scotchie's water and kibble bowls and put out the big guy's breakfast portion of wet food, I headed downstairs and climbed on the treadmill, jacking the incline all the way to the top, since I'd have to get my burn in intensity rather than time.

With some good pop music, I was able to get moving and generate enough endorphins to wake myself up. I was feeling almost good—and wishing I had more time—as I hopped off and threw an old purple sweatshirt over my yogas and tee.

Almost walked into Michael at the door.

"All yours," I said, planting a quick kiss on his cheek.

He pulled me in. "You too."

"If I didn't have to finish packing lunch, I'd take you up on that." I detached myself and swatted his backside. "Have a good walk."

From there, it was nonstop.

One thing after another after another as I rushed through the preparation and the school run. Daniel couldn't find the right socks and I had to rummage in his drawers and peel the missing one off a different sweater. Michael left a trail through the house, from bagel crumbs on the counter, to a sweaty T-shirt in the hall, to a wet towel on the bathroom floor. Adding insult to injury, I was pulling into the lot when Madge texted me pics of three different pink ribbon bows with the caption "Thoughts?"

Oh, I had thoughts.

Things didn't get any better outside the car.

Corinna snapped at me when I asked how she was, then apologized, explaining she'd spent the whole morning fighting with Imani. It apparently started with a minor dispute about shoes and quickly became the kind of barn-burning ugliness thirteen-year-olds can spark. Okay, so she won for worst start to the day.

Or she did, until Brian arrived, looking tired and walking Zooey with unusual care.

"What happened?" Corinna and I asked in unintended unison.

"Zooey was playing around on the floor by the stove, somehow got ashes in her eye and scratched her cornea." Brian shook his head. "She's already most of the way healed. I'm exhausted after spending the evening at the urgent care."

"No wonder," I said.

"Tough night," agreed Corinna. "Imani did that once, and after the first night, the only real issue was the antibiotics. She hated it."

"Zooey too." Brian sighed. "Gonna be a long ten days."

"Got that." I shook my head.

"I told you we'd need a lawyer!"

Kryssie clattered up behind us, already dressed for the day in another long beige wool jersey dress under a camel-colored coat. I was sure the cognac leather boots cost more than a week of my legal services.

"I'm sorry?" I asked, cringing inwardly as I felt a chunk of my hair creep free from the scrunchie.

"The police called. They want to talk to me."

"It's standard," I assured her. "They're probably just going down your contact list and getting everyone who was there."

"They called us last night," Corinna said. "Just wanted to know what we saw and where we were when Eric Egan fell."

"Left a message at the store while I was with Zooey at the urgent care," Brian added. His tone was just a tiny bit too casual as he continued. "Took about five minutes. Probably get to you today, Grace."

Or my chat with Lieutenant Luciano at Craft World counted. Equally possible.

"Well, I don't need this right now," Kryssie said. "I'm working with the counselor today and…"

I had a glimmer of an idea to back her off. "Kryssie, it's actually good to have all the documentation."

"Documentation?"

"Well, if you decide to pursue some kind of action for the emotional distress, you'll be glad to have police records of where you were at the time, and what happened."

"Action?"

With a silent prayer for forgiveness and protection for the aquarium, I nodded. "Well, people do occasionally sue over emotional trauma."

Kryssie's eyes gleamed. "Really?"

"Yes. I don't do that type of law, but I know it happens."

"Do you know—"

"No, I don't," I said, in a brisk and definite tone. "If you need a criminal attorney, though..."

The comment brought her up short for the critical instant it took for the bell to ring and the kids to start crowding to the door. In the crush, we managed to evade Kryssie and head to our vehicles, offering each other the supportive eye rolls and smiles friends do on this kind of day.

We'd get through this, and tomorrow would be an easier day. Right?

CHAPTER FIFTEEN
...AND ONE MORE THING

Finally. Done.

Back home, I took advantage of the quiet to enjoy a long, hot shower without anyone wandering into the bathroom and demanding attention—of any description.

I started to think maybe I was going to get a good morning to clear some work—even sneak in a nap before pickup.

Wrapped in my towel, enjoying the warmth of the steamy bathroom, I took the time to slather on some of my favorite lavender body cream, getting a deep breath of the soothing aroma. Maybe the nap first...

And then, of course, my phone rang.

I muttered a curse under my breath and opened the bathroom door just enough to grab the device, then closed the door to keep in the warmth. "Grace Adair."

"Hey, Grace! Sorry to bug you on a mom day."

Annie Guzman, our paralegal and mother of a toddler, was well aware what busy moms might be doing in their rare and precious "me" time.

"Not a problem," I said. "It's you. What's up?"

"There's a man here who wants to see you in reference to your clients Kaufman and Scupper."

"Al and Vince?" I asked. State's Attorney's Office internal affairs? Police pension board? Angry relative? Nothing good here.

"His name is Ethan Storey." Annie knew enough of the background of the case to know it was a bomb—but she dropped it in her usual cool and professional tone.

"Really?"

"Yes. I've told him you aren't in the office today, but he asked me to call you and see if it's all right to give him a number where he might reach you."

"If he can wait half an hour, I'll be there in person."

"Since he was offering to wait until Michael got back from a motion hearing, I think he'll be cool."

"Great. Just give me time to put on some shoes."

"Boots."

"What?"

"We had some thaw and re-freeze in the night and the sidewalk's a mess."

"Thanks for the heads-up."

I hit End and took a last longing look at the purple velour three-piece leggings, tank, and cardigan set I'd been looking forward to wearing on this slow day. Maybe when I got home from pickup.

I scrambled into black jeans, a cream-colored pointelle tee, and a purple wool blazer, adding a pair of lug-sole Chelseas so I wouldn't go flying on the ice. Flick of mascara, swipe of lipstick, and ready to go. Not court wear, but acceptable enough. Puffer coat because it was barely twenty degrees.

I noticed as I got in the car that Michael's white dress shirt was still hanging in the back seat. I'd forgotten to drop it off at the cleaner's—I could do it on the way back. *Had* to do it on the way back. He only had one full-dress shirt, and there was no acceptable substitute.

In the car, I put on my favorite "mom music" radio station

and listened to the DJs interrogate a couple about a bad first date. He thought she was crazy, she thought he was a jerk—and nobody thought there'd be a second spin. As far as I could tell, the entertainment value resided in making married people thank the good Lord they were no longer single.

Every day, baby. Every. Single. Day.

I was joining the DJs (happily married, but not to each other) in a nervous laugh over the whole thing, when I looked down and saw it.

The check engine light.

Just in case my day wasn't lousy enough.

Great. Somewhere in here I'd have to find time for a trip to Neil, our local mechanic. Unless I could palm it off on Michael…

Since he fancied himself a bit of a car guy, he might be willing to handle it, just because he liked talking cars with Neil. And if he'd been in a motion hearing all morning, he might well be glad for an excuse to knock off.

I pulled my dark-blue sedan next to Michael's shimmery red Infiniti and started up the walk—and was immediately grateful to Annie for the warning and the lug soles. Building maintenance was usually very good; Michael had taken a long-term lease on the third floor of the repurposed store during a dip in the market, and now it was some of the nicest office stock in New Haven.

Probably just bad timing on the re-freeze. I was sure they'd get to it by midday.

As usual, I took the stairs, always glad to grab a little extra exercise.

In the office, Annie was at her desk, working on some kind of document, with the phone to her ear. Typical morning for her.

Her black eyes rivaled the sparkle of today's glasses, lipstick-red rhinestone cat-eyes. "Did you get a speeding ticket?"

Annie flicked a brow toward the waiting area, where a thin man in his thirties was sitting on the edge of one of our comfortable deep-blue chairs. He was wearing a battered navy-blue parka over jeans and a gray flannel shirt, with tan work boots. Everything looked like it had been worn in when he got it, but it was clean and carefully maintained, as was the man himself, his dark hair shorter than usually seen in New Haven, his pale face clean-shaven with no hint of scruff. His hands, folded between his knees, suggested the precision was more than just a personality quirk: the nails were bitten to the quick, a couple showing angry red lines as if he'd been gnawing on them.

Maybe a bit less composed than we thought.

"Mr. Storey," I said, holding out a hand as I walked toward him.

He stood, the way nicely-brought-up men are still taught to do, and half-extended a hand. "Are you..."

"I'm Grace Adair. Mr. Kaufman and Mr. Scupper's attorney." I decided the matter for him, reaching for his hand for a quick, but firm, shake.

"Nice to meet you." His tone suggested otherwise.

"Why don't we go in the conference room here and chat?" I suggested, as I motioned to the door.

"Thanks." Ethan Storey flinched and looked, if possible, even more awkward when I opened the door for him and motioned him inside. I suspected whoever taught him to stand for ladies emphasized door holding as well.

"I promise I won't tell your grandpa you didn't hold the door," I said.

"How did you..."

"It's the kind of thing a man teaches a boy, and you're following standards that are at least a generation old, so I guessed."

"Guessed right, Mrs. uh, Ms. Adair." He blushed, which only made his grayish pallor seem healthy. Even by the standards of pale people in midwinter, he was washed out, with bruise-like purple smudges under his light eyes.

"Either is fine. As long as people remember to call me Counselor in court, I don't care." I gave him a smile. "And it's good to know a few years in the drop-off line hasn't ruined my observation skills."

He returned the smile, tentatively, then stood awkwardly just inside the door.

"Please have a seat. Would you like some coffee? It's good Italian roast."

"Ms. Guzman offered me some," he said, shaking his head. "I try not to drink too much caffeine—makes it hard to sleep."

"Understandable. Herb tea, maybe? Everyone needs something warm on a day like this."

Ethan Storey stared at me for a moment. Then: "Um, yeah, if you wouldn't mind."

"Of course I don't. I'm a mom. I tend to everyone." I shot him a grin.

He responded with another faint, nervous smile.

In the minute or so it took to set him up with a cup of lemon-hibiscus tea and offer honey, which he declined, I watched him carefully. People give away all kinds of things if you know what to look for. Ethan Storey certainly did. He was terrified. Of me, for sure. There was a lot more to it, though. The flash of longing when I offered the sweetener, and the quick assurance that he didn't need it pointed to someone who could not enjoy simple pleasures—or could not let himself enjoy them.

Considering who he was—or more accurately, who he'd been about twenty years ago—it was interesting.

I made myself a cup of coffee, took a nice deep breath of the rich steam, and sat at an appropriate distance from him, giving him another reassuring smile.

He didn't return it, setting down his cup and meeting my gaze sharply. "Why are you being so nice to me?"

"Why wouldn't I be? Kindness and politeness are about me. About how I treat other humans made in the image of God. Everyone deserves a certain basic level of respect."

Ethan Storey's eyes widened a bit. "I believe that too, but I don't always get it."

"I can't control what other people do," I said, taking one more sip of my coffee before putting it on the table. "Which, I suspect, brings us to why you're here."

"Yes and no."

I waited.

"I know you, and your clients, know who I was. You know what I did—really, what I didn't do—that night. I stood by and let it happen, and didn't try to break it up or get help."

He broke off, took a breath.

His story to tell.

Finally, he met my gaze with surprising strength. "I can't make it un-happen. But I served my time, and I've spent the last fifteen years trying to make the world a better place. I work for Haven Home, helping people get off the street. Volunteer to mentor other ex-cons—I don't bother with that 'formerly incarcerated' stuff. Live with three rescue cats and feed ferals because I can't stand the thought of anyone or anything suffering or hungry."

"Impressive."

"No." He shook his head. "Just trying to be a decent human. Like I couldn't be that night."

"Ah."

"I'm not that kid anymore."

"I know," I said. "No one is who they were twenty years ago."

"If you live, you learn," he said. "I'm lucky. Maybe too lucky."

I got it, then. The guilt. He'd never forgiven himself. "I'd guess that's not for you to decide. Me either."

"What about your clients?"

"Ethically, there's very little I can say to you about them, or on their behalf."

He winced, then nodded.

"That said, I will tell you I believe as a matter of principle that pursuing vengeance does no one any good. And that I am in the habit of urging all my clients to avoid repeating their offenses."

A bit of the tension in his shoulders relaxed. "Oh."

"Speaking strictly for myself, Mr. Storey, I think you've done a tremendous job of rehabilitating yourself, starting with acknowledging the harm done, and continuing through your efforts to help others."

"You don't have to say that."

"I happen to believe it." I held his gaze. "I also think that you've given yourself a life sentence, which perhaps far exceeds the interests of justice."

"What do you mean?"

"I mean, maybe you need to talk to someone who could help you to stop torturing yourself. If you don't even feel worthy of honey in your tea, how can you enjoy anything in your life?"

"I'm not meant to enjoy…" he started.

"Not for you—or me—to say, Mr. Storey." I shrugged. "Please take care of yourself."

"What are you going to tell them?"

"Precisely what I told you I would. That they should make every effort not to repeat their offense."

"Thank you."

I nodded.

"You're not what I expected, Mrs. Adair."

"Find me someone who's exactly what you expect, and I'll find you someone who's pretending. You're not as expected, either, Mr. Storey…and that's all to the good."

"Thank you." He picked up the tea and started to take a sip, then lowered it. "Do you still have that honey handy?"

"Here."

"Thanks." He drizzled a bit into the cup. "You know, I honestly don't know how that night went so wrong."

"No?"

"No. I read the reports later, so I know now what Char had planned. But I didn't know then—I thought we were just going out to the lake to drink like usual. The other girls knew something was up, but didn't know how bad it was going to be. Char's boyfriend—I guess he just went along with whatever. And Ronald…"

"What about Ronald?"

"He egged them on. He's the one who told them to cut her hair." Ragged breath. "I was hiding in the bushes, trying to get up the guts to run for help, and I looked up and saw him, watching the girls scratch and beat her—and he was all—um, excited…sorry, Mrs. Adair. Sorry to be gross."

"It *was* gross," I said. Understatement of the year.

"Sometimes I wonder what happened to him."

"You don't know?"

"No. It's weird. He just disappeared from the face of the earth after serving his sentence."

Not weird at all, I thought. If, God forbid, I'd been Ronald Doremus's mother, I'd have had him change his name and move across the country. "Probably got a new identity."

"So he could be anywhere…or nowhere."

I nodded.

"World would probably be a better place if he weren't in it," he said. And then, suddenly, sharply: "Sometimes I think it might be better without me too."

"That's not up to you, Mr. Storey," I said.

"That's what Mother Michael says."

"Who?"

"Cathie." Ethan blushed more noticeably, his posture turning awkward and squirmy. "She joined a contemplative order of nuns."

"Nuns?"

"Yes. She's Mother Michael of the Angels at the Contemplative Priory over in Old Weymouth."

"Wow." I drank a bit of my own coffee. "How…"

"She wrote me a long letter maybe seven years ago, telling me she forgave me and would pray for me. I write to her every once in a while now. She's like…kind of a guardian angel, you know?"

"I do." Better than I'd ever tell him. And his revelation gave me, finally, a solid idea to stop Al and Vince once and for all. "It's good for both of you that you've found peace and forgiveness."

"She's found peace. That's what counts." He drank the last of his tea. "Thanks, Mrs. Adair. You've been really helpful and kind."

I stood, and he followed suit, again showing those old-school manners.

"I'm going to do everything I can to back off my clients," I assured him.

"Thank you."

"It's just time for this to end. Everyone involved has—"

"Not everyone, Mrs. Adair. I'm not sure what happened to Ronald…"

True enough. And now I had to worry about whether he was lurking somewhere just outside the frame. At this exact moment, though, I could send Ethan Storey on his way with a little reassurance and get to work on my plan.

Which was exactly what I did, exchanging a few sentences of

friendly chat about the New Haven social service scene. Turned out his path had crossed with a friend of mine, Corinna's old boss Moira, now an outreach worker at KidsRead, the literacy group. Connections made, I saw him to the door.

As he walked toward the stairwell, Michael stepped off the elevator.

"Who?"

"Ethan Storey," I said.

"*That* Ethan Storey?"

"Yup."

My husband's eyes widened a bit. "Well, then."

"He's not who I thought he was—and probably not who Al and Vince think he is either."

"Yeah?"

"Definitely not the big bad of the piece," I said. "Tell you more tonight."

"Sounds good. I have another motion hearing in an hour."

"And I have to get somebody's shirt to the cleaners," I said with a wink. "Plus, the check engine light is on."

"Check engine?" His face suggested concern, but there was a certain little-boy gleam in his eyes. "Probably needs to get looked at."

"That's usually what warning lights mean."

"Oh, fine," he said, reaching in his pocket for his keys. "I guess I can stop by the mechanic on the way home."

"Thank you, dear. I'll pick you up if need be." I gave him my keys and shot Annie a smile. We both knew that put-upon tone was actually cover for happiness at getting to go talk cars with a pal.

"I'll let you know." He held my gaze with just a little bit of intensity. "Be nice to my car."

"Am I ever anything else?"

"No." Sheepish smile, and then he pulled me in for a quick kiss before I dashed out the door.

As I ran down the stairs, I went over my list of things to accomplish before pickup. It was a lot, but I could do it.

Too bad I didn't get the chance.

CHAPTER SIXTEEN
EXIT GRACE

Michael's car is an amazing thing.

He bought his first shimmery red Infiniti soon after his initial big trial win, when it became clear the solo practice was a going concern. But he bought the sedan, not a sports car, because we were expecting Daniel, and he was every bit as thrilled about being a dad as he was about being a successful gunslinger.

Now he's on the second one, even more shimmery and cushy than the first, with all manner of bells and whistles I don't—and don't want to—understand. But still chosen so it'll hold Daniel's booster seat in the back.

I'm not really comfortable driving the thing, honestly, but on the rare occasions they're offered, I take the keys with a smile. He's the only man I know who happily allows his wife to drive his car.

Corinna's husband, Clay, will pay for a rental before he'll let her take his, and he's far from alone. So I always feel very lucky when I slip behind the wheel and settle into the smooth black leather, smiling at the color, because he chose black over beige with Daniel in mind.

There's nothing wrong with my car. It's a very nice deep-blue sedan, not high end, but definitely not entry level, with a bunch of little niceties like seat heaters. We bought this one because it has the highest safety ratings and easily accommodates most models of booster seats. And it definitely handles like a mom car: solid and intentional, nothing quicksilver here.

Michael's car, though, handles like a sports car. It's designed specifically for someone like Michael: a dad who wants to have some fun while being responsible.

So it always takes me a few minutes to get adjusted to the handling. I usually turn too hard and overcorrect at least once. But once I settle down, it's fine.

I'd left my car unlocked, not the smartest choice ever in New Haven, even in the daytime, but good because I had to get the shirt. As I hung the shirt in the back of Michael's car, I heard a honk and squeal and saw a pickup truck peeling away from the corner, the driver flashing the universal sign of disdain. I didn't see the other vehicle, but I was willing to bet it was one of the standard near-crashes that happen dozens of times a day around here.

I just hoped I wouldn't be in one.

The last thing I needed was to explain to Michael how I got into a fender bender in his car.

Too bad there wasn't an irony alert light on the dash.

Thanks to road construction—the official sport of Connecticut—I had to take a different and longer way back to Alcott, going farther down toward the Sound and then working my way back up. It was starting to feel pretty good driving Michael's car, and I'd found my favorite radio station, which happened to be playing a recent Taylor Swift song I liked. I'm not a hardcore Swiftie, but I do enjoy a lot of her music…and all of her feisty attitude. I was singing along with the chorus when I noticed a large dark SUV a bit too close behind me.

Weird.

This little traffic work-around was unusual, and nobody but

locals should have been here at this time of day. As I made the last turn before the on-ramp, onto a back street right by an inlet, I wondered what was going on. The SUV was awfully close.

Maybe someone on their way to the hospital? The Yale New Haven ER was on the other end of town, but if they were lost—

BANG.

The SUV rammed my back bumper.

I swore, swerved, and hit the horn. "Watch it, buddy!"

As I got my bearings and pulled straight, the SUV hit me again. And this time, it wasn't a bump.

It kept pushing. Trying to run me off the road.

In my own car, with the steering I was accustomed to, it might have ended differently. In Michael's car, with that sharp, slick handling, I pulled away, veering toward oncoming traffic…and almost immediately overcorrected.

When I whipsawed back into the correct lane, the SUV was waiting for me.

It didn't take much.

As I fought for control of the car, the SUV gave me one more push.

This time, I hit my head on the steering wheel. Ow.

Cursing like Tony Soprano on his worst day, I tried to straighten the wheel.

Only when I heard the buzz of the tires hitting the warning grooves at the edge of the road did I look up and realize where I was.

And what was coming at me.

Sparkling in the cold winter sunlight, the water of the inlet looked deceptively beautiful.

I slammed on the brakes, tried to turn away.

Too late.

With a surprisingly soft splash, the car went into the water. Kept going.

And going.

I'd driven past the inlet hundreds of times. Never thought to wonder how deep it was.

Deep enough, as it turned out. Probably why it wasn't frozen.

I broke off halfway through a particularly colorful curse.

This was going to be bad.

Really bad.

All right. No panicking. There'll be plenty of time to panic later.

I hope.

How do I get out of this?

Staying in the car and waiting for help just didn't seem like a good option. I remembered a famous 1970s water crash where the victim was found with her head at the roof, clearly desperately trying to survive until help arrived.

No thanks.

Looked like I would be swimming for it. Michael and I both had one of those tools that can cut through a seatbelt and break glass. And hopefully the rescue squad would be here before the hypothermia got me.

Hypothermia would be faster, anyhow.

I grabbed the glass-break tool out of the console. Hit the seatbelt button and was pleased to discover that it still worked.

Good omen.

I'd take all the help I could get.

I kicked off the heavy Chelsea boots, got rid of the puffer— the instant it got wet, it would be dead weight.

Must be a better way to put that.

One more big, deep breath while I still could. I looked away to protect my eyes.

Okay, here we go.

I smashed the tool into the sunroof. And everything exploded. If cold can explode.

I wasn't sure what was broken glass and what was frigid water as it all came rushing in at me. But I managed to keep my focus on getting up and out.

Cold. Cold to the point that it was like burning alive in reverse.

Climbed through the sunroof. Felt a scratch on my leg as I went, flinched, but didn't stop.

Couldn't stop.

Still not at the surface.

Something white—is that the light? No. Michael's dress shirt waving in the current.

Flash of him in full dress on our wedding day.

Over there—light?

This wasn't the clear Caribbean water of Daniel's fish documentaries.

Bet it smelled terrible.

Hoped to find out.

Can't hold my breath much longer.

Kyrie eleison—

No! Keep fighting.

Somewhere up there is my kid.

Up. Which way is up?

Archangel Gabriel intercede for us…

Come on. I've got enough fat to float, don't I?

Try—find a way up…

There had to be a way out.

Had to!

I'm not leaving Daniel…not leaving Michael.

So cold.

Kyrie eleison, Archangel Gabriel intercede for us…

CHAPTER SEVENTEEN
WATER LANDING

NEW HAVEN COUNTY POLICE AND FIRE RADIO TRAFFIC:

"Hamden Rescue—car off the Water Street cutoff—into the inlet. Send Fire and EMS."

"Water landing?"

"Affirmative. Front end submerged, trunk just visible, but sinking."

"Fire and Rescue on the way. Any further info?"

"Red Infiniti, vanity tag N-T G-L-T-Y"

"Tag, Unit 20?"

"Tag: Not Guilty."

"Not Guilty?"

"Copy."

"New Haven Duty Sergeant here. Did you say the tag was Not Guilty?"

"Affirmative, ma'am."

"Rolling to the scene, Dispatch."

"Copy."

"Dispatch, the car's almost fully submerged. Warn EMS—it's going to be a water rescue."

"Any sign of the driver?"

"Not yet."

MOTION HEARING, NEW HAVEN DISTRICT COURT

M ichael Adair, the lawyer you call when you're *really* in trouble in New Haven, was trying to convince Judge Clement Howland to throw out a key piece of evidence against his client when the clerk saw something on her screen and turned to the judge.

"Adair, could you please approach?"

"Of course, Your Honor."

"Clancy informs me the Hamden police are trying to find you. Apparently, there's been an accident. They've taken Ms. MacInnes Adair to Yale New Haven."

Later, Michael wouldn't remember how he got out of the courtroom or onto the elevator. All he'd remember was running into Vince Scupper in the lobby.

"I was just coming to get you, Adair. Grace was in a crash."

"I know. How—"

"Don't know yet." Vince motioned to the door. "I'll give you a ride to Yale."

"Thanks."

In the car, the older man watched Michael as he buckled up, his hands a little shaky as he tried to control his breathing. Michael checked his phone. A text from Annie, saying the same thing Judge Howland had said. An accident. Grace. The police were trying to find him.

"What the hell?" Michael asked the phone more than Vince.

"Someone ran her off the road. In your car," the older man said, looking sharply at him. "You know anything about that?"

"What?" Michael stared back, blindsided.

"Well," Vince said, turning out onto the street, "there are only two possibilities. Either you were the target, or you set it up."

Michael took a breath. Tried to process what Vince was saying. He knew Vince didn't like him, but he had no idea how Vince could even think he'd harm Grace.

Grace. Tweety. The love of his life and mother of his son. The other half of his soul.

"If you weren't driving, I'd slug you," Michael said finally.

Vince, damn him, let out a dry, nasty chuckle. "Good answer, Mike."

"What?"

"You're all right for a hired gun. I had to ask. So we'll assume you were the target."

"Because it was my car," Michael said, his voice wavering as a hole opened up somewhere in his midsection, the realization hitting hard. This was meant for him.

"And also because, with great respect to your wife, she's mostly a mom right now. She's not out in the world enough to have any exposure."

"So it has to be me." He folded over, rested his head in his hands.

"Sorry, son, I'm afraid it does." Vince patted Michael's back as he took another turn. They were only a couple of streets away now. "Offend anybody lately?"

"More than usual?" Michael rubbed his face, sat up. His stomach still hurt. Everything was off balance. Wrong.

Everything would be wrong until he could look into Grace's eyes.

If he could.

Vince guided his car into the visitors' traffic circle at the Yale New Haven Hospital. "Look, the cops are going to ask you about this. Probably pretty soon."

"Yeah."

"Pal, I know what this is like." The older man stopped the car and met Michael's gaze dead-on. "My wife got hit by a drunk twenty years ago. It's hell."

"Got that."

"Keep your eye on the ball. If you keep your mind on the practical stuff, you won't fall apart."

Vince's voice wobbled a little on the last two words.

"She's—" Michael started and broke off.

"She is. My wife was everything to me too." Vince smacked his arm and pointed to the door. "Now get in there and make sure she's okay."

CHAPTER EIGHTEEN
ON DRY LAND

Kyrie eleison, Archangel Gabriel intercede for us…
Warmth. Very good.

Not too warm. Even better. I probably wasn't in hell.

"She's going to be fine, Mr. Adair." Cool, professional voice. Probably the hospital.

That had to be good. And Mr. Adair meant Michael.

As good as it gets.

"I want *her* to tell me that." Michael's tone was sharper than usual. I registered it, but far more important just then was the fact that he was holding my hand, his warm fingers laced with mine.

"Michael, I'm fine." My voice came out weak and rusty, but recognizable. I opened my eyes.

The first thing I saw was Michael, his green-and-gold eyes burning into mine, the connection between us as strong and immediate as it had been the first time we saw each other in the law library almost twenty years ago.

This.

This is where I belong.

"Tweety." His voice wobbled a little on the second syllable, and he bent toward me.

I pulled him in. Only when I tried to wrap my other arm around him did I realize I was connected to an IV.

"What—" I started.

"Mostly for the hypothermia, Mrs. Adair." The cool, professional voice was attached to a woman about my age, with smooth, dark hair in a sensible ponytail, and big brown eyes. "That's always a major risk with something like this."

Michael squeezed my hand again and pulled back, taking a breath and trying to get back to game face as much as he could.

"Right," I said. While I was awfully glad to be alive and in one piece, it seemed to be taking a tremendous amount of work to process things. "Am I okay?"

Dr. Kakar, as her name badge identified her, smiled a bit. "You will be. You have a mild concussion, a nasty cut on your shin—probably from the glass—and mostly minor scratches on your face too. Plus a bunch of bruises, and of course the hypothermia. Nothing that won't heal with a little rest and time."

"Good." I nodded, and my head hurt. "Concussion."

"Yes. It's normal to feel a little disoriented after a trauma like this, anyhow, and you may have some brain fog for a while from the concussion." She moved closer, pulling an examining light from her pocket. "I'm going to check your pupils and—"

The light slashed through my eye, and right through my skull.

"Ow."

My stomach lurched and twisted. For an instant, I thought I might throw up.

"Light sensitivity," observed Dr. Kakar in a matter-of-fact tone. "Happens sometimes. You're probably spending a few days in a dark room once we send you home."

"When will that be?" Michael asked.

"We'll keep her for observation tonight because of the concussion and hypothermia, and you can take her home in the morning."

"Good."

"Daniel's still at school, right?" I asked. "I need to call Corinna."

"You're okay unless he has a short day," Dr. Kakar said. "It's only noon."

"Noon?" I blinked, trying to place myself in space and time.

"It's okay." Michael hadn't let go of my hand. "I'll get Daniel."

"Good." Suddenly, embarrassingly, I was crying. Not sobbing or anything, just quietly oozing tears. I needed to hold my little boy.

Michael's fingers tightened on mine. "Can I bring him to see her?"

"Sure. She'll be out of the ER and in a room by late afternoon."

"Good. I'll bring him right from school…maybe with a stop at the candy store." Michael shot me a grin, as the nurse walked in and the doctor out.

A round, bright-eyed woman, she took an appreciative look at him, and grinned too, at him, and then me.

"You're right, honey," she said. "He is an angel. Hi, Gabriel."

Gabriel. The prayer. The nurse heard me saying the *Kyrie.* Hopefully that was all she'd heard.

Michael flinched as if he'd been slapped. "My name is Michael. Michael Adair. I'm her husband."

"Oh, well." She shrugged. "Must be some kind of misunderstanding."

She went through a quick check of my vitals and slipped out, shooting one more look at Michael on her way.

Uncomfortable silence.

"Tweety, who's Gabriel?"

Oh, hell. "A prayer—the Archangel Gabriel."

"Why…"

"Oh, my mother believed in some old superstition about the Archangel Gabriel protecting abandoned daughters."

Michael studied me for what seemed like a very long time. Long enough I worried he might know something he shouldn't.

Then he squeezed my hand. "Abandoned daughters."

"Yeah."

My father had left when I was small, and my mother, honestly, was probably happier without him. I'd come through with surprisingly few daddy issues. Though at that exact moment, I did want my mommy. The mother I'd buried in my last year of law school.

More tears oozed out of my eyes.

"I'm sorry, Tweety."

"I'm okay," I said.

Michael laughed. A wild, hard, inappropriate sound. "The hell you are."

Our gaze held for a long moment.

"I love you."

Unintended unison and perfect understanding at once.

I was still holding his hand when I dozed off.

The rest of the day was about as fun as you'd imagine. More tests, more lights in my eyes, and more questions about what day it was and who was president. (Bad enough having to answer that one *once!*)

It was late afternoon when they finally wrapped me up in a couple extra blankets and wheeled me to a room upstairs. By the time I was settled, I was exhausted again and drifted off once more.

Hoping I'd wake to Michael and Daniel.

Bitter disappointment there.

When I woke again, a tired-looking youngish woman in a basic gray suit was sitting in the bedside chair.

"Mrs. Adair?" she asked.

"Yes."

She flashed a badge. "Detective Vigliotti, New Haven PD."

"Nice to meet you."

"I'm told you were in the SA's office at one point. I didn't get my shield until two years ago."

"Yeah, I was a prosecutor. Worked with Vince Scupper."

"And now you're a defense lawyer with your husband?"

Edge in her voice. Great.

"When I do legal work," I said. Equal edge. "Usually, I'm a mom and run a small editing and fact-checking business at home."

"Oh." Vigliotti absorbed that. "So…any idea who'd want to run either of you off the road?"

"I'm sure there are people who don't like us for any number of reasons." I took a breath. It was a lot of words to get out at once. "I don't know of anybody who'd hate us enough…"

"Well, you're still in shock. You can think about that a little and get back to us."

"Okay."

"I'm just going to ask you a few routine questions, and we'll leave this for now, okay?"

"Fine."

"Everything all right with your husband?"

"Yeah. We're fine. Actually made it to the fun part—our son is six, and we get to sleep again."

"Wish I did. My twins are fourteen months."

That explained the tired look. "It gets better. Promise."

"I'm going to hold you to that." Vigliotti managed a smile and returned to her checklist.

"You feel safe at home, right?"

"Of course."

"Hell, yes, she's safe at home."

The voice cut into our quiet conversation like a lash.

Michael.

"Ma! Daddy took me to SweetHeart's after school!" Daniel rushed into the room and threw himself at the bed. "I got gummy worms!"

Whatever composure I'd had, and whatever was left on Vigliotti's checklist, the presence of my baby shattered everything the way Michael's sunroof had exploded into a million pieces a few hours before. Only this time, what broke apart was me.

I pulled Daniel close in a desperate hug, buried my face in his hair, and unraveled into a huge, embarrassing ugly-cry.

Daniel snuggled in, patting my arm and assuring me that everything was just fine. Quite a stand-up guy, my little fella.

At the edge of my vision, I was aware of Michael and the detective exchanging a few words, not happily. But that was about all.

Anything anyone else wanted would just have to wait.

CHAPTER NINETEEN
SHE HAS TO ASK

"Whoa. I want to see the other guy."

My Saturday began with Lieutenant Carla Luciano standing in the doorway of my hospital room. I was alone at the moment because my roommate was getting some kind of test. Fine by me.

She'd been a joy all night. Despite the partition, her snoring and gastrointestinal eruptions were more than loud enough to keep me awake. And nauseated.

Not to mention the floor noise. Dings and rings and bangs, intercom announcements and more. I tried to listen to the TV on headphones, but it didn't help much.

Michael and Daniel had stayed until the end of visiting hours and left with a promise to return and scoop me up as soon as they were allowed.

Luciano had to have planned an early visit to catch me before they arrived. I wondered why she was taking over for

Vigliotti. Unless something had changed dramatically since my prosecuting days, brass didn't usually get involved in direct investigative work.

Must be something extra going on here.

Play along.

"Yeah, I kicked his butt," I said, starting to smile, until the cuts and bruises on my face twinged.

"You're here, so it's a win." She gave me that little nod police give each other, and occasionally prosecutors, as an affirmation. "Not sure I'd have had the brass to break that glass and swim for it."

"Had to get home to my kid." I motioned to the bedside chair.

Shrug, and then she sat. "Yeah, I'd have taken my chances with the water for mine too."

"Exactly."

We let that settle for a moment.

"Any thoughts on who might want to come after you? Or your husband?"

"Because I was in his car." I started to nod, and it felt like my brain was sloshing around. Even less pleasant than it sounds.

"Exactly."

"Could be anything. At any given time, he's defending a bunch of not-great people."

"How not-great?"

"Well, it's a matter of public record. We do all kinds of serious cases—and somebody might be unhappy about the outcome."

Carla absorbed that, chewing lightly on an index fingernail, an adorably girlish gesture. "Heard through the grapevine that you two have some kind of connection to Don Nunzio."

"Not quite," I said. "Just getting his sister's daughter into drug court and rehab."

"Oh. Way I heard it, Michael was taking some kind of mob case."

"Nope." I sighed. "No chance the guy who told you that was a uniform unhappy about how the case went?"

Luciano looked down at her hand. "Could be."

"Well, it's really a textbook drug court case. Nineteen-year-old girl shoplifting for drug money—got hooked after a bad injury. Nice kid, decent background, no violent history…"

"But?" The lieutenant's warm brown eyes sharpened on me.

"She was scared out of her mind and tried to bite one of the officers who took her in. So they're probably not thrilled she ended up in drug court and rehab."

"I can see that."

"You know I wouldn't have tried for it if she'd really bitten him or hit the officers."

"You wouldn't have gotten it anyhow."

"True."

Shared, rueful smiles.

"Still," she said, "you can't discount the idea somebody really was trying to send a message to the Don."

"Maybe."

"Or maybe the girl's dealer isn't thrilled that she's going to be on the right path and they're going to lose a good client."

"Also possible," I admitted.

Luciano nodded, taking a long look at my face. "It's superficial, but you definitely took a beating out there."

"Gee, thanks."

"It's really okay. I took some glass frag at a scene years ago, and it healed just fine."

"Yeah?"

"Yeah—I'll get you the info on what I used."

"I'd appreciate that."

A few seconds of surprisingly comfortable silence.

"So you came out this morning to offer beauty tips?" I asked.

"Well…" Her expression suggested I'd caught her. "Actually, my daughter has dance class this morning. And I figured, since we have a bit of a rapport, and we're not getting much of anywhere…"

"You'd see if you might get something?"

"Honestly, figured you might trust me with something you wouldn't feel comfortable talking about with Vigliotti. She's awfully young."

"Seemed smart, though."

"She is. But grown-ups know things."

"We do." I held her gaze. "Unfortunately, I don't know anything much about this, other than that a big dark SUV slammed into my trunk."

"And that's really all?"

"That's really all."

"Okay." Luciano nodded, holding eye contact. "While we're having a lovely conversation about uncomfortable things, have you heard anything further about Al and Vince's little crusade?"

"No," I said. Ethan Storey's worries were not evidence of anything. "But they could still go freelance."

"I sure hope not."

"You and me both."

"Losing his pension and getting sued would be a pretty lousy wedding present for Al," she said.

"Yeah, and the last thing anyone wants is Vince forced into retirement."

We shook our heads together.

"Fingers crossed they continue to lie low."

"Your lips to God's ears," I agreed. My turn to prospect for info. "You heard anything about the aquarium death?"

"Not sure if you know this, but Eric Egan has a bit of a history."

"The parish in New Jersey?"

"Yep. Details turned up when we did the standard victim check." Her generous mouth tightened in distaste. "Of course, nobody deserves to be dumped in the beluga tank…"

"But if somebody had to be…"

"He's a pretty terrific candidate. Exactly. Don't get me wrong, we're doing all we can to sort it out. But if somebody on that train recognized him from his earlier…*misdeeds*…we'd have a very hard time convincing a jury to vote for murder."

"Might even be hard to convince the state's attorney to go to bat," I said.

"Guess it would depend on who was making charging decisions on the given day. Let's just say we want to clear this, but we'd be open to hearing about extenuating circumstances."

"Understandable." I thought of Brian and Pete on that little train, up above the water. They swore they were watching over Zooey. But how could they not see something—or someone? And what if it wasn't just seeing?

"Are you hearing anything?" Luciano asked.

"Nothing concrete." God's honest truth there, at least. "A lot of people didn't know the background."

"No?"

"There was a little word on the street that he was a bad guy who shouldn't be near kids. No specifics."

"The kind of thing somebody might put out if they'd acquired knowledge by confidential means and couldn't breach confidentiality, say?"

"Pretty much."

She held my gaze. "Somebody was risking a bit for a good cause."

"Yup."

"You're a stand-up lady, Mrs. Adair."

"Darn right she is."

"Ma!"

Daniel blasted into the room, as Michael stood in the doorframe.

"I don't think we've met," Michael said.

My visitor stood, hand out for a shake. "Lieutenant Carla Luciano, New Haven PD. Your wife and I have a few mutual acquaintances."

"And a few mutual interests," I added, holding Michael's gaze. *I'll explain later.*

Shaking Luciano's hand, he said, "Well, Lieutenant Luciano, I'm sure you won't mind if we get my wife home so she can recover in a much more relaxing environment."

"Happier, I'm sure," said the lieutenant, giving Daniel a bright smile. "I'm not sure more relaxing."

"In its own way," I said, "chaos at home is the very best medicine."

CHAPTER TWENTY
SAFE RETURN?

Within an hour, I was tucked into the passenger seat of my car, wrapped in my raincoat over an oversized fleece, my biggest and darkest sunglasses covering my face, with a sheaf of release instructions and warnings in one hand, and a large ginger tea from the coffee cart in the other. In the tsunami of concern and advice Michael had fielded since the crash, there'd apparently been several mentions of ginger tea for the concussion nausea. He latched onto it as some kind of panacea, arriving with the big cup in hand, and proudly assuring me there were three boxes of different kinds of ginger tea and a new jug of honey in the car.

His obvious joy in doing something for me made me smile, and I was still chilled enough to appreciate the hot cup, so I didn't have to fake a positive reaction. Even if my stomach was still doing flip-flops every time I got close to a light source.

Not to mention the exhaustion. Dr. Kakar had warned me

fatigue would be an issue, and that was before the lovely and restful experience of sleeping alone in a hospital bed.

I assumed I'd eventually stop being insanely grateful to see Michael and Daniel every time they walked into the room, but it wasn't going to happen that morning. Michael had proudly brandished the tea and a bag of clothes clearly grabbed from the top of the Salvation Army pile, which he sheepishly admitted mistaking for the fresh laundry pile only after he'd packed the bag.

The black sweatshirt and gray joggers were the last of my post-pregnancy clothes, found in a drawer during a recent cleanout, but they were warm, which was almost enough.

Fortunately, Michael had taken the underwear from the right drawer, and while the pieces didn't match either the outfit or each other, they were relatively current. The shoes were nice too: the fuzzy-lined clogs I wore for the school run, exactly the comfort I needed.

Lord love him, he'd even brought a scrunchie—a shiny silver polka-dot one—so I could make some sense of my hair. I'd gathered it into a pony and turned to the mirror to be sure it was neat...and sat back down on the bed, hard.

I'd known I would look rough. I hadn't known *how* rough.

Deep smudges under my eyes, common for a concussion, were only the beginning. There was a big dark bruise on my left cheekbone, and too many bloody little scratches to count. The only really bad ones were over my right eye and at my jaw. Saying I was a mess would be an insult to messes.

"Oh." I took a breath. Suddenly I wanted to cry. I hadn't been all that hung up on my looks—I thought. But this...

"Tweety, you are still the most beautiful woman I've ever seen." Michael rubbed my back. "And all of this will heal."

"Superficial, right."

"Right. Most of it will look better in a day or two."

I took another cautious look. He was right—the little scratches would fade quickly, and the eyes might look better after a couple nights' rest. "But the bruises..."

"Mama, you're still pretty." Daniel had sat down on the bed beside me and gave me another hug.

And I, of course, had teared up yet again.

Michael put a hand on my shoulder. "You'll get good makeup. I'm sure you—or one of your friends—knows enough about cover-up to do it."

"Probably true." Add that to my list. I was sure there were a slew of tasks waiting for me as soon as I was able.

"C'mon," he'd said, holding out my raincoat. "Let's just get you home."

"Not the worst idea you've had."

I let him wrap me up, and Daniel took my hand.

On the ride back to Alcott, Michael gave Daniel his phone, so he'd be busy and absorbed in something other than our conversation. The drive was pretty fast for a Saturday midday, even though he took the main roads, deliberately skipping the short-cut where the crash had happened.

Not that it mattered.

The knowledge of the last time I was in a vehicle filled the car as surely as water had filled the Infiniti.

Michael tried for resolutely practical, assuring me he'd filed the report with the car insurance company, and reeling off details: He was taking this car to Neil the mechanic today, my replacement phone would arrive Monday, we'd pick up the rental car Tuesday, he'd ordered new credit cards, but I'd have to start the paperwork for a replacement driver's license myself, and my friends would be coming to check on me every couple hours.

"They will?" After that glimpse of myself in the hospital room mirror, I'd hoped for another day before anyone saw me.

"They will. I have to get ready for the voir dire next week, and they've been blowing up my phone, so…"

"Okay." He was right. I'd been on the other end of this a few times. Sometimes, letting a friend be there for you is important for the friend.

"And I don't want you alone for too long."

I heard it.

"You think somebody's coming for you."

"Well, I doubt they were coming for you, Tweety. It was my car, and I'm the one who's out there."

"I'm out there too."

"Not like me. And who would know it was you? They'd have to be following you and waiting for an opportunity. Which…"

"Really scary." I looked out at the highway ahead. "But also really unlikely."

"Exactly." He took my hand, keeping his eyes on the road. "I'm sorry."

"You didn't send them after me."

"Vince Scupper thought I might have."

I laughed. It was the only possible response. Daniel looked up at the sound, shot me a smile, and returned to blowing up candy or jewels. "Vince doesn't know you very well, does he?"

"Guess not." His attempt at a dry tone failed miserably. "Sorry, Tweety. It really bugged me that he'd even think…"

"He didn't, really. He was being protective of me and testing you a little. Typical old-school guy."

"I guess."

I squeezed his fingers. "Nobody else—including the police—even entertained the thought."

"True."

We were at the exit for Alcott, and he was silent as he turned off and drove down the connector.

"I just keep thinking, what if you hadn't gotten out of the car…"

"But I did. And we'll figure it out from here."

"Okay." He didn't sound convinced, and I was sure it was far from the end, but neither of us had the energy to pursue it further.

At the house, I walked in carefully, gingerly. Scotchie met me and licked my fingers, but didn't try to pin me to the wall—he obviously sensed I was vulnerable.

I'd put down the release instructions, and the still full and tepid cup of ginger tea, when my knees turned to water.

I sat down on the couch like a broken doll.

Michael stared.

"Mama?" Daniel asked.

"Just tired, sweetheart," I said. "I'm okay. Really."

"Sure you are."

"I'm okay enough to sit here under my afghan while you two go to the mechanic."

"Actually, the gang's coming over for just a few minutes as soon as I tell them it's okay."

"Really? They want to see me like this?"

"Hate to tell you, Tweety, but people love you."

"Not everybody, though."

Michael took my hand and held my gaze very deliberately. "You are safe. Whatever this was, it almost certainly has nothing to do with you. Got it?"

"Got it."

"Good. Now, Daniel wants to see his pals, and their parents need to see you."

My head hurt at the thought of three kids and two more grown-ups in the house.

"For ten minutes. Just to be sure you're fine and bring you a few things, okay?"

"Okay."

In the event, it was much better than okay. Corinna brought me a basket of herbal bath products—clean and organic so there'd be no problem with my healing cuts—and Brian brought a heated blanket, a comfort I had not even known existed.

The sound of our kids laughing in the dining room while we talked was exactly what I needed after everything. If I happened to notice that Brian seemed unusually tense when I asked how he and Corinna were doing, at that point I wrote it off as concern for me.

It was only later, when I dozed off and dreamed myself back to the Aquarium, watching the beluga whale twirl through the water, that I remembered I still didn't have a good answer for what he and Pete had been doing that deadly morning.

Just then, though, it drifted out of my battered brain with no more interest or value than the little current in the wake of the whale.

CHAPTER TWENTY-ONE
TEA AND NEW TROUBLE

Sunday morning began pretty much where Saturday ended—with me in a heap on the couch. I'd awakened in the middle of the night, with my head and the cut on my leg throbbing, and wandered out to the bathroom for a couple of aspirin.

Then sat down for a moment because I didn't want to wake Michael.

Daniel found me there at dawn, followed pretty quickly by Michael. They dragged me back to bed with them for a while, and then when they got up, I went back to my spot.

Which is where I was when the doorbell rang as Daniel scrambled into his shoes.

"Hey, you two!" Madge was at the door, with a gift bag and a big plastic carry box. "I'll take it from here, Michael."

"Thanks, Madge." He hugged her, planted a kiss on an uninjured spot on my face, petted Scotchie, then turned to give me one more kiss before bugging out for the hardware store.

Yes, one might suspect the fellas would prefer church to express gratitude for my lucky escape—but honestly, they probably needed the store and Old Man Loquat's bracing presence more than sitting through a service. I knew they'd thanked the Higher Power for my survival in their own way and I wasn't going to push.

"You planned this, didn't you?" I asked Madge.

"Of course we did." She held out the bag. "Something nice to wear while you're recovering."

"Aw, thanks." I indicated yesterday's sweatshirt, thrown over my pajamas. "It was nice of Michael to bring me this, but..."

"Goodwill pile?" she asked.

Shared laugh.

"And I probably shouldn't be wearing black right now," I said.

Madge studied my face. She hadn't reacted when she saw me the first time, to her credit, but now, her eyes widened. "Yeah, you need a few days. It looks superficial."

"It is, but it's going to be ugly getting there." Suddenly, I realized something. "I'm not going to heal by the wedding."

"You've never heard of makeup?" Her voice was calm, even if her expression was a little tense. "You have enough time for everything to heal over a bit, and you'll be able to cover it. So you'll be a little more radiant than the average flower girl..."

I managed a laugh.

"Now, go shower off and I'll heat up the cinnamon rolls."

My stomach wobbled at the thought of eating, but I just nodded. No point arguing.

"Oh, and Michael tells me there's ginger tea."

"There's a lot of ginger tea. Ginger lemon, ginger peach, ginger mint..."

"Good. I'll make you some and you can sip it while we talk."

"Tell me we're talking about the seating chart."

Madge's face turned serious. "Why don't you just get cleaned up."

Twenty minutes later, I was wrapped in a very nice purple knit two-piece outfit—Madge has discovered online lounge clothes and same-day shipping—with a mug of ginger-lemon tea in my hands, and a cinnamon roll in front of me. For Madge's sake, I'd taken a couple of bites and was allowing it to settle.

Which so far it was, thankfully.

My stomach didn't stay settled for long, though.

Madge set down her mug and took a breath. "Anything from the police?"

"Nothing. An old friend of Al's checked on me yesterday morning. She's starting with the idea that that it might have something to do with us defending Don Nunzio's niece."

"Really?"

"It's the only recent thing we're both involved in, and more importantly, a lot of people don't like Don Nunzio."

"But families are usually off-limits unless they get involved, right?"

"Usually. But the girl's been using, so she could have come up against something nasty."

"Someone who doesn't like that you're taking away his business."

"Exactly." I took a sip of my tea. I don't love the stuff, but it's warm. "I actually hope it's an angry drug dealer."

"Easy answer, and he's sent his message."

"Right. Because if it's not, it could be anyone on Michael's client list."

"Or yours." Madge held my gaze.

Oh holy hell. I almost dropped my mug. "You don't think…"

"I can't see how. But after this, I'm terrified I might have missed something."

Not an unreasonable fear when you're a member of a centuries-old order of assassins. But there was absolutely nothing pointing anywhere other than Michael, and/or my legal work with him.

Though, of course, I wouldn't necessarily see it.

"Understandable," I said finally. "But I really don't think so."

"And you're not crosswise with Professor Munroe over my marriage, are you?"

The mug did wobble in my hands at that. I set it down hard on the table, splashing my hand.

"Ow." I wiped my skin on the edge of the heated blanket, stared at her. "What are you saying?"

She shook her head, patted my arm, practically falling over herself. "I'm not, honey. I'm just scared about everything right now."

I just looked at her. The lawyer truth-serum gaze.

"I know you, Grace. I know you'd go pretty far for a friend and I was just worried..."

"I'd like to think I'd get some warning if I'd gone that much too far."

"I'd like to think you would too."

"You don't *know*?"

"Well, there are questions that never come up, you know." Madge squirmed a little. "You left things well with Professor Munroe, right?"

"I did. And I have a plan to fix this. I was getting ready to set things in motion when I—"

"Right. I'll tell Professor Munroe you're recovering and back on the case."

"Okay."

She heard the edge in my tone.

"Grace, I'm sure you have nothing to worry about from that quarter." She rested her hand on mine. "Absolutely sure. You'd know if you did."

"I would, wouldn't I?"

"Indeed. We move slowly and carefully, after all."

We sat for a while longer, sipping tea. Madge didn't argue about my not eating the rest of the cinnamon roll. I think she knew my stomach upset was a bit more than the concussion.

CHAPTER TWENTY-TWO
COMFORT DUDES

The concussion did make me tired enough to nap after Madge left. A couple hours later, I was dozing through an episode of my favorite procedural (yes, I love *SWAT*—fight me!) when the doorbell rang. Pete Hurley was standing on the stoop with a blue gingham hot/cold bag.

"Hi." Not really a surprise, I supposed. Corinna had church, and Brian had the Sunday afternoon rush at the hardware store, which was a religious experience all its own—and of course Michael and Daniel's hangout too. Pete had to be the designated hitter.

No disrespect intended to him, of course—he's a good guy and fits in really well in our circle, a big part of why we were all hoping he and Brian would get together.

"Hey." Pete winced a bit as he got a good look at my face, but didn't remark on it. "I'm told you're supposed to be checked on by a responsible adult every few hours. And I'm way better than the usual responsible adult."

"No argument here. Please come in."

He grinned. "I come bearing gifts from Team Stein. Bubbe's Jewish Penicillin, Zooey's chocolate chippers...and Uncle Pete's Common Crackers. Brian was worried you wouldn't be properly fed."

"Well, thank you."

Within five minutes, we were settled in front of the TV with bowls of soup, and Pete was showing me what to do with the crackers. They're a New England delicacy, kind of like giant oyster crackers. You split them, butter them, and dip them in the broth.

It's even better than it sounds.

Especially if you've barely eaten for days, and food suddenly smells good again.

"Wow," I said after my first bite. "These are amazing."

"They make everything better." He beamed. "It's a nice mix, though. Classic New York chicken noodle plus New England crackers."

"Nice mix like you and Brian," I said and immediately regretted it. The concussion had knocked down my boundaries a little.

"Yeah." Squirm and blush.

"Sorry."

"Nah. It's a good point. You know my intentions are honorable, right?"

"You don't have to convince me."

"I have to convince Mr. Loquat, though. And any good word helps." A sheepish little shrug. "This whole thing kind of surprised me."

"Love has a way of doing that," I said. "Did I ever tell you I planned to be a US Attorney or Supreme Court justice? Never figured I'd marry, never mind be a mom. Even when I was carrying Daniel, I fully expected to hand him off to an excellent, properly vetted daycare and return to my professional life."

Pete smiled at me over his bowl. "So what happened?"

"Life." I shook my head. "You don't really know how you're going to feel about someone—or something—until you're there. Daniel was almost a month old when Michael ran the numbers and said I could stay home, if I wanted to. And I couldn't imagine doing anything else. It wasn't easy, or comfortable, for a while, but it was right for us."

"Good for him too," Pete said. "Kids really do better with more parent time if you can give it to them."

"Yeah. With the store, Brian's able to be there for Zooey, and it makes a huge difference, especially considering the loss."

"Definitely. He's an amazing dad."

I recognized the note in his voice. "I loved Michael before we had Daniel, but seeing him as my boy's father makes me love him more. I'm guessing Brian's parenting skills are a big point in his favor."

Pete blushed as only redheads do.

I'd been too blunt…those loose guardrails again. "I'm sorry. I shouldn't—"

"Oh, you nailed it, Grace. I'd love to marry him and help raise Zooey. I'm just scared, after everything."

"Life is pretty damn scary." I patted his hand. "But hiding doesn't do anything other than deny you a chance at happiness."

"How did you get so wise?"

"Easy to tell other people to take a risk," I said, taking another cracker. "Brian's crazy about you, Mr. Loquat thinks you're great, and Zooey thinks you're the best thing since glitter."

He laughed. "High compliment indeed."

"They're very sparkly at that age."

"It's a magical age," Pete said. "They're just starting to be individuals—and the world hasn't really gotten to them yet."

"True." I heard something in his tone and looked up from the cracker I was dipping in my soup.

"What is it, some kind of lawyer truth-o-meter?" he asked.

"Nah." I shrugged. "Studying people is a huge part of my job. I have to know when somebody isn't telling me something. I'm sorry. It doesn't turn off."

Pete put down his bowl.

"You don't have to tell me anything," I said. "None of my damn business."

"I wouldn't mind talking about it, if you wouldn't mind hearing it."

"Of course. Least I can do." I put down my soup too.

"I was thirteen. Dad left Mom for a while, and things were just bad at home."

"Tough age, even when everything's great," I said.

"Yeah. Even more so if you're hoping to grow up and marry a nice fella."

"People were a lot less cool then."

"They aren't always cool now," he said. "But it's better."

I nodded.

"And Mom, God love her, thought church was the answer."

I knew, then, where we were going. "Oh, no."

"Oh, yeah. He was the junior pastor. Thought I was one of the cool kids when he asked me to come watch baseball with him and the priest at the rectory..."

"I'm so sorry." It was the only thing I could offer. Well, unless I wanted to bring in the sisterhood for some pro bono work.

"Yeah." Pete toyed with his spoon. "So, you can imagine how thrilled I was when I found out what Eric Egan had been up to before he was a curriculum consultant."

"How—" I hadn't realized they knew that much.

"Matter of public record. Brian got an off vibe on the guy, and then you warned him, so he ran him through the background check system the store uses for prospective employees." Guilty shrug. "Probably abusing the system, but..."

"Don't ask me what happens under the table in law enforcement, and I won't ask you about what happens there."

"Fair enough." A wry little smile. "You get it."

"Sure do. I don't think anyone—other than Egan's mother, if she's still alive—was sorry to see him leave this earth."

"Nope." He turned the spoon in his fingers. "Brian would have gone to the school board if Egan hadn't—"

"I'd have joined you." Of course, it wouldn't have been an issue for long, considering my assignment. But one day could be too long with someone like that.

"We didn't know he was going to be on the trip," Pete said. "Zooey asked us both to come, and of course I was thrilled. Then when we saw him, we made sure we were in the same group."

"Good call." My mouth said it, even as my battered brain screamed for him to stop telling the story. I did not want guilty knowledge.

"And then, well…"

"What?"

"That's the crazy part," Pete said, just a little too quickly. "Zooey's seatmate was fussing, saying she was going to be train-sick, so we were focusing on her. I didn't hear anything until the splash. Brian said he thought he might have heard a grunt first, but that's it."

It matched my own experience. It was also a tiny bit too perfect. But I couldn't be 100 percent sure on that. And I definitely didn't want to know something I'd have to deal with in some way. Especially since everyone agreed the right thing had happened.

Maybe not the *way* it should have happened, but the right thing for sure.

"That's about what I heard down below," I said, reaching for my soup bowl. "I hate to be insensitive, but you're absolutely right, the world is a better place without that guy. And it's a sin to waste good soup."

Pete's nervous expression melted into an adorable smile. "Well, we can't have that."

"Nope."

The soup was gone, and we were happily watching a wedding competition show, with Pete nitpicking the venues and flowers, and me critiquing the dresses, when Brian arrived.

The fellas exchanged glances, and then hugs, since they were in a private family environment, and Pete took off.

Brian accepted a cup of coffee and sat down to chat for a bit.

"How are you, really?" Brian asked.

"Better than expected. The concussion is no picnic, but I'm here and mostly okay."

"Good. The first we heard of it was from Kryssie, and she made it sound really bad."

"Kryssie?"

"A firefighter friend of hers apparently heard it on the dispatch."

"A firefighter friend..." I broke off in giggles, and so did Brian. Kryssie was well known for her fondness for the emergency service. Let's just say it's not civic-mindedness.

"Good to hear you laugh. You know, you look pretty rough."

"I'm putting my faith in makeup."

Brian shrugged. "Honey, unless it's spackle, I'm not your guy."

"Not the worst idea ever."

"Oh, shut up." He laughed, "By the way, brace yourself for a busy evening."

"What?" I asked cautiously.

"It's not bad. We got a new shipment of those wonderful handmade 3D wooden jigsaws."

Daniel loved the puzzles from a business started by a local Iraq war vet who'd reinvented himself as an artisan. They were good-sized things in varnished light wood, beautiful and elaborate, usually dinosaurs or fantastic creatures. It took most of an evening to build one.

I could think of a lot worse ways to spend the night. "What's this one?"

"Loch Ness Monster. Michael took one look and fell in love."

"Of course he did. Anything Scottish, you know."

"Is he wearing the kilt for the wedding?"

"Oh, yeah. Between him, Al's friend the reserve general, the assistant commissioner, the judge, and the rabbi, it's going to look like the Village People."

"All we need is a leatherman."

I gave him the serious mom glare. "Don't get any ideas."

"Nah. I don't want to scare Pete...or my great-uncle."

"You don't—"

"Don't ask a question you don't want answered, Counselor."

Good advice—on so many levels.

CHAPTER TWENTY-THREE
PRACTICAL BUT NOT MAGIC

Building the Loch Ness monster did indeed take all evening. Which was just fine.

It kept us all busy until bedtime, with a short break for a simple dinner from the air-fryer: chicken nuggets and fries, practically dump and go. But cooking mattered to me. Sure, the basics were all I could handle, but honestly, they pleased my guys as much as any number of more elaborate meals.

Once Nessie was happily swimming atop our coffee table, we tucked in Daniel, only to have him pop up and tuck me in. Also fine by me. While we weren't dwelling on it, he had to know his mom had been in some level of danger to sustain the injuries I had.

If it made him feel better to tend to me, I'd take whatever fussing he wanted. It would be a very long time before I'd take a hug and kiss for granted from anyone I love.

Deep in the night, when Daniel was long asleep, I woke to Michael wrapping his arms around me. I snuggled in, glad for the closeness, and quickly fell back to sleep, his breathing the last thing I heard as he buried his face in my hair.

Next morning, it was Monday, and time to start easing back into the practicalities. Michael handled drop-off, and Corinna offered to bring Daniel home, so I could spend another day in the house before I started getting back into the world.

Michael asked me if I wanted to speed up the car rental paperwork, but I honestly didn't mind going without wheels, so we left it for Tuesday.

The fellas had just left when the delivery person arrived with my new phone. If I expected to return to the world at all, I had to be connected. Whatever the smartphone folks tell you, we all know that getting a new phone up and running is a time-consuming and frustrating task. Even less fun with a concussion and the attendant brain fog.

My mental acuity was somewhere between "Is my heated blanket on?" and "Find the right show to binge," and these people wanted me to reel off strings of numbers and follow menus. Of course they did.

Eventually, with the help of a very kind customer service person who took pity on me, clearly assuming I was about a hundred years old and ever-so-slightly cracked, I got the thing up and working.

While it beeped, booped, and bobbed as the messages and alerts from the weekend downloaded, I got myself another cup of tea, this time ginger mint, and looked over the Sunday paper Michael hadn't bothered to read. New Haven wasn't exactly a news desert, but we weren't a thriving print market either.

Still, I should not have been surprised to see the story in the lower-left corner of the local page: Local Attorney Injured in Water Crash.

I was, in fact, the local attorney in question. Just a few sentences, with the note that I'd been taken to Yale in stable condition and the police were investigating the possibility I'd been run off the road. The reporter wasn't a complete dunce, because she pointed out I was in a car registered to my husband, "the high-profile defense lawyer" involved in several controversial cases. The pic was probably more disturbing: Michael's Infiniti being pulled out of the inlet, battered and ice-frosted, with a big divot in the back. Fortunately, they didn't have any pics of me from the scene. Bad enough they printed my age.

Great. So not only do I care more about my looks than I thought I did, I'm also more hung up on my age than I expected. Any other ugly surprises about myself?

I folded the paper and moved on to the next task: putting an outgoing message on my email explaining I had a concussion and would be slow in responding for a while. Probably get me a box full of new concerns and questions, but at least everyone would know what was going on.

Then, on to the DMV to start the license-replacement process. How much more fun could my life get?

I quickly found out when the phone had finally loaded all my messages.

Fortunately, more than half were alerts from news sites I follow, with updates on the latest messy political controversy in which I currently had less than zero interest. The others were mostly clients and friends, in varying degrees of annoyance, and later concern, as they tried and failed to reach me. Most folks got a quick return text: "I'm doing fine, recovering from a nasty car crash, and I'll get back to you as soon as I can."

A couple of the messages weren't so easily handled.

Two from Professor Munroe. The first: "Call me when you have a chance, Grace. We need to get some clarity about your plan to handle matters."

It would have chilled my blood even before the crash. Now? I wrapped my hands around the mug of tea and tried not to shudder.

Her second message was far gentler. "I'm sorry to hear of your trouble. Spend a few days recovering and we'll speak again. Margaret is keeping me apprised of developments and looking to your safety."

No wonder Madge was nerved out. If Professor Munroe had given *me* a similarly phrased assignment I'd be worried too. After all, Madge had even less of an idea what had happened to me than I did—and she was now responsible for making sure

I was safe. A great big "or else" was implied in Professor Munroe's always-careful phrasing.

I'd better get back in the game soon.

The next pair of messages only confirmed my feelings and raised a whole new set of concerns. They were from Ethan Storey. The first, the night of the crash, was an apologetic plea for me to talk to my clients, because he'd seen Vince and Al driving by again.

And there was no way he was mistaken or overly imaginative, because they were in Vince's Bonneville. A 1958 copper and ivory model, which is supposed to be garaged in the winter. He'd recently snapped up the car, getting a deal after it figured in a murder case. I could only conclude Vince would try to claim he took the car out for a spin and happened onto Ethan's street.

Not sure if that was brass or stupidity.

Either way, it sure didn't help.

How was I going to assure Professor Munroe that Al and Vince had learned their lesson? They'd just ignored everything I told them at Ersalesi's and their promise to me.

Ethan Storey's second message didn't help: "Mrs. Adair, I'm really sorry I bothered you earlier. I just found out what happened to you. I'm sorry. Please let me know if there's anything I can do. I'll worry about Mr. Scupper and Detective Kaufman later. Just stay safe and get better."

What a kind person, I couldn't help thinking. *What a decent man.*

Whatever he'd been that night at the lake, he seemed to have become a good human.

And I had to pull those two old cranks off his case.

No option.

I sent Ethan Storey a quick text thanking him for his concern and promising to address the issue.

Then I called Al.

"What the hell did you think you were doing?" I snapped when I heard him pick up.

"Grace? Are you okay?"

"I'm fine. You may not be if you and Vince keep blasting around New Haven in his damn Bonneville."

"Oh, crap."

"Oh, crap indeed. You two promised me you'd back off. You *promised*. And now I get a call from Ethan Storey telling me he saw you in his neighborhood?"

"I'm sorry. We're just—"

"You're not just anything. You're violating conditions of your release, endangering your case…and really ticking me off."

"Okay, well."

"And not for nothing, Ethan Storey has become a decent man. He's spent the last decade and a half trying to atone for what he did, and he doesn't deserve you two mopes driving around his neighborhood waiting to catch him littering."

"Mopes?" Al chuckled.

I wanted to kill him. Good thing this was a phone call. "Mopes. I'd use stronger language, but I don't want to teach you any new words."

"Sorry, Grace, it just sounded funny when you said it. We really were just out running Vince's car when we got the idea that—"

"Don't get any more ideas!" I stabbed the End button.

Not nearly as satisfying as hanging up used to be back in the day. But it would do.

I dialed Vince.

Got his voicemail.

I could still work with that.

"Drive your damn Bonneville anywhere you want, Vince, but don't go near Ethan Storey's house. This is formal legal advice from your very annoyed attorney."

Then I cut off sharply again.

Scotchie let out a little whine.

"I'm not mad at you, big guy. Need a little air?" I asked. I took him out to the front yard, figuring the next snow would take care of any unpleasant consequences. On the way back, he barked at the bushes by the house.

"What's wrong?" I asked.

He barked again, and I looked, but couldn't see anything. He must be having the same day as the rest of us. Definitely some kind of craziness out there in the ozone.

After all the drama, I was absolutely exhausted.

Zero energy to deal with the imaginary terrors Scotchie was seeing in the bushes. Whatever it was, it would be there tomorrow, or it wouldn't be, and then it wouldn't be my problem.

Be awfully nice if *something* wasn't my problem, I thought, as I collapsed on the couch.

CHAPTER TWENTY-FOUR
WITH A LITTLE HELP...

A few minutes after three, Corinna showed up with Daniel and Cherise—and thankfully no baked goods. Even better, she had a to-go tray from Louisa's, with two big dark roasts, black, as the good Lord intended.

It's wonderful to have a friend who knows you.

After Daniel tackle-hugged me and Cherise handed me an adorable get-well card she'd made in art class, we settled the kids with Madge's leftover cinnamon rolls and milk and adjourned to the living room for a good catch-up.

"You are my hero," I said, popping the tab on the coffee. "Everyone's been feeding me ginger tea because it's supposed to be good for the nausea."

"Is it?"

"Sometimes. Mostly just staying out of bright light seems to be the best thing."

Corinna nodded. "My mom and grandma went after me

with the ginger tea both times I was pregnant. It does kind of work, but it gets pretty old."

"Michael's just grabbing at straws. Trying to help because it makes him feel better."

"Oh, I know that one. When I fell last year, Clay was bonkers for the first week. They don't realize how much they depend on us until something happens."

"Got that." We shared dry smiles. Corinna had fallen on the ice in the grocery store parking lot and suffered a nasty sprained wrist. It had slowed her down for a couple of weeks and probably scared Clay.

I caught her looking at me.

"How bad is it?" I knew she'd be honest.

"Oh, it's bad. But it doesn't look like anything that won't heal."

"Thanks. People keep trying to pretend it's hardly noticeable."

She shook her head and took a sip of the coffee. "No, honey. It's noticeable and ugly. But it's not forever."

"I'll take it." As she lowered her cup, I clinked mine against hers. "Got a few days till the wedding, and there's always makeup."

"Good thought. Right now, get as much rest as you can because it'll help with the eyes." A wry twist to her mouth. "And Michael won't be playing perfect husband for long. Clay was back to the usual benign neglect inside a week."

"I figure that's about all I'll get."

"You might get another day or two for the water landing."

It was supposed to be a laugh line, but I found myself suddenly almost weepy.

"Oh, Grace—I didn't mean..."

"It's not you. It's the stupid concussion." I drank a little coffee, took a breath. "And you're right, I'd better work it while I can."

"With this crew, absolutely." She took my hand. "You okay?"

"I'm going to be." I squeezed her fingers, let go. "It was pretty scary for a while, but I'm here, and that's what matters."

"It is."

"Well, that and good coffee…"

We clinked cups.

"Brian and Old Man Loquat send their best, by the way."

"Hopefully, I'll get to the hardware store soon."

"You and everyone else. That storm in the forecast for next week has everybody a little bonkers."

"Of course it does."

"JakesPop was asking after you too."

"Him? Jeez, I'm surprised he noticed I was gone."

"Right?" She laughed. "He's usually so useless. But he saw Michael walking Daniel up and asked what happened."

"Nice of him, I guess." I shrugged. "Probably worried he'll have to do more work at the next Parents' Room Day if I'm out of commission."

JakesPop's laziness at the monthly events was legendary. Corinna shook her head. "He might actually have to open a box."

"He could end up in the hospital from the effort."

We were laughing when the doorbell rang.

"Brian?" I asked.

"Nope. Last I heard, he had some kind of paint emergency again. Somebody from the McMansions over on Leighton needs the precise shade of buttercup yellow."

"Hooray for the real housewives," I said, as I looked through the peephole. "And speaking of real housewives…"

Corinna looked as surprised as I felt when I opened the door and Kryssie Farrar minced in. She was carrying a Cake-Safe from one of those fancy overpriced kitchenware lines that you see on the shopping channels. It was pale blue, covered in cheerful yellow flowers with white script scrolling around the outside. I could make out "for you."

"Here." She shoved it at me. "You look horrible."

"Well, thanks," I said, taking the surprisingly heavy piece. "Nice to see you too."

"It's a butternut squash bundt with orange glaze. Loaded with antioxidants for healing. From Alyssa Marchand's website—you know, that wonderful health influencer."

"Um, great." I did not think the light reflecting off the snow was the only reason my stomach was turning a slow cartwheel. I took a breath and tried to be polite. "Thank you so much, it's very kind of you."

"Yeah, whatever. Why didn't you tell me about Eric Egan?"

Well, that's an interesting question.

"I'm sorry?" As soon as I'd found out about Egan, I'd given Corinna and Brian a very carefully worded warning and urged them to quietly share it as appropriate.

"I just found out where he really came from," she huffed. "Why didn't anybody tell me before I said all that stuff about what a good guy he was?"

"The information was out there," Corinna said. "Grace heard a little something through legal channels, and I ran a public-records background check. We didn't make a big deal about it because he could have sued us."

"Sued?" The word ended in a squawk.

"Yes." I set the cake down on the table by the door. "People have brought suits over things like that being shared around. And I couldn't—and still can't—explain where I got the information without violating my ethics code."

No need for anyone to know which profession's code.

"Well, fine. I still look like an idiot."

A small movement of Corinna's jaw told me she was doing exactly the same thing I was—biting her tongue to prevent herself from saying what she was thinking.

"Kryssie," I began gently, "it was a tough situation. Nobody's going to blame you for offering a few appropriate words."

"No?"

"Not a one," Corinna agreed. "You had to be civil. You couldn't go up there and say, 'The world's a better place without this fool,' even if it's true. Not while you're talking to parents who may or may not know all the details."

"And," I added, "it's not just polite, it's safer. Any defamation claim would die with Egan, but his family could have claimed some kind of emotional distress if it got out that you'd trashed him publicly at the PTA meeting."

"Oh."

"They wouldn't get far, but it would be a pain in your backside." I gave her a very deliberate look.

Whatever message I'd intended—and whatever she'd meant to respond—evaporated as she got a good look at my face. "Wow. You're really—"

She broke off, probably unable to think of a word bad enough to describe it.

"It's superficial," I said.

"Cuts and bruises," Corinna added briskly. "No permanent damage. She'll be fine in a couple weeks."

But, I realized, I'd better stay out of court until I healed. At the very least, the bruises were distracting. At worst, they might make me seem less credible because a judge or juror might think I wasn't competent to be working. Or that I couldn't handle my own life, so how could they trust my word on a client?

One more way I'm grounded, I thought irritably.

"Anyhow, Kryssie," I said, "thank you so much for the cake. It's very kind of you. I apologize for not offering you coffee, but I've got a lot of fatigue from the concussion and…"

I trailed off, hoping she'd get the subtle message: LEAVE.

Unfortunately, subtlety was lost on Kryssie.

"Well," Corinna said, standing up, "I should probably collect Cherise and get moving. I need to get everyone clean and fed and set up so Clay can cover during the budget meeting."

"Thank you for bringing Daniel home," I said, focusing on her as if Kryssie had already left. Maybe that would work.

"Look, I understand you're tired," Kryssie said. "But I'm still trying to figure out this Egan thing. You know he came highly recommended, right?"

Well, that woke me up. "Really?"

"Yes. What I heard was that the head of his company personally called the superintendent to suggest him."

Now, that was interesting.

Corinna and I exchanged glances.

"What company?"

"IntelliStrong Curriculum Solutions." She glared at us. "It's only in the bulletin and the board minutes and—"

And any number of other things I'd never bothered to read, I thought. As soon as I could stand some screen time, I was going to be checking out the company.

"Okay," I said. "I think the easy answer is the same one it always is in a small town: connections. Egan knew somebody who knew somebody."

"Probably," agreed Corinna, with about as much pleasure as I'd offered the explanation. Since neither of us were from, or allied with, the incestuous little Alcott power structure, we weren't fans. Kryssie, however, as an insider's insider—just ask her—should have known better.

"All right, fine." She forced herself to look back at me. "I'm really glad you're okay, Grace."

"Thanks."

"Well, I heard from a firefighter involved—um—someone who knew, that it looked pretty bad when it happened."

"It wasn't fun," I agreed. Still, I'd have had to be in much worse shape not to appreciate Kryssie's reference to a firefighter. We all know our beloved PTA leader is also the sweetheart of the emergency services. She goes through firefighters like the rest of us do chewing gum.

Corinna shot me an eyebrow.

"So you're actually very lucky," Kryssie said, returning to her default setting of aggressive perkiness. "Even with all—that—on your face."

"Probably. Folks at the scene thought it was bad?"

"Yeah. Apparently, they were calling the dive team when you popped up screaming...you don't remember?"

"Nope. Don't remember the crash, either."

The corner of Corinna's mouth twitched. She knew what I was doing. How better to protect myself than to get the word out that I had no idea what happened? And couldn't identify a potential attacker.

"Well, that's probably just as well. Who wants to think about being in that freezing, dirty water?"

"Not me, for sure." Corinna patted my arm. "Didn't the doc tell you a lot of people never r emember this kind of thing?"

"Yeah. Fine by me, honestly."

"So they don't know who did it?"

"Who did it?" I asked.

"Well, word from the scene"—unconscious and unintentionally damning stroke of her hair—"was that there were SUV tracks showing somebody ran you off the road."

"Hmm…" I drank a bit more of my coffee. "Well, I guess I'll just add this to my own list of traumas and keep on going."

This time, now that she'd dropped all her bombs, Kryssie did take the hint.

"Well, I'm glad I brought you the bundt—the antioxidants will be especially good for your skin. And don't forget to get to your derm. It wouldn't hurt you to get a peel and a little filler anyhow, and once there's the scar tissue…"

I managed a smile, with a little side-eye to Corinna. In addition to everything else, Kryssie had confirmed most of our suspicions about her look.

Wait till we got a chance to talk to Brian.

"See you at drop-off tomorrow!" Kryssie chirped. "Hugs!"

Corinna and I stared after our dear princess for a moment, the way you do when a speeding train has passed. Then she motioned to Cherise, who was finishing a very intense round of tic-tac-toe with Daniel and picked up her own coffee, clinking it against mine.

"Speaking of adding it to the list of traumas…"

"I think I'm going to need a spreadsheet."

CHAPTER TWENTY-FIVE
DINNER FROM THE DON

T hat evening, we got another surprise—and questionable pleasure.

Michael came up the walk carrying a huge delivery bag from DiStefano's, one of the best Italian restaurants on New Haven's Wooster Street, and a box from Ersalesi's.

"Good idea," I said. "I'd have been happy to throw something together, but..."

"I didn't do it," he replied, his face tightening a bit.

"No?"

"Don Nunzio sent it to the office, with his compliments. I think he's going on the assumption that you were targeted because of his niece."

"Oh, hell."

"Yeah, pretty much."

"Daddy!" Daniel blasted into the living room and tackle-hugged him.

I took the bag and box into the kitchen. The fragrance of

tomatoes, herbs, and rich slow cooking immediately filled the room. I realized I hadn't eaten since a couple of bites of left-over cinnamon roll early in the day, before the sunlight started bouncing off the snow, and my stomach growled. As I unpacked the bag, I couldn't help laughing.

It was chicken parmigiana.

Presumably, Michael wouldn't mind eating DiStefano's version.

The package also included pasta, a tray of Caesar salad, and a loaf of garlic bread. Enough for about six people—by Italian restaurant standards—so we'd be fed for days.

If we didn't mind Don Nunzio buying us dinner.

"Wow," Michael said, as he walked into the kitchen. "Smells amazing."

"It does. You're willing to eat *this* chicken parm?"

He had the grace to give me a sheepish shrug. "Special case."

"Fair enough." I held his gaze. I didn't have the energy to fight, but he needed to know I was choosing not to.

"Bigger problem is where it came from."

"Which of us is sending the thank-you note?"

Faint smile. "Oh, you are."

"I'll make it a combination note. I didn't have a chance to write the one for the flowers before…"

"Yeah." Michael opened the garlic bread, pulled off a piece. "I think we accept with thanks and stay careful. The Don is probably sending us a message."

"Which is?"

"Well, you know I clerked with the feds, and I have a friend left in OC."

The fact that he was referring to his old law school pal, now an organized crime prosecutor, suggested real concern.

"I do."

"Well, I called him after the New Haven detective asked me if I knew anyone who might be especially unhappy with me."

"When did that happen?"

He finished chewing a bite. "The other night at the hospital, while you were hugging Daniel."

"You mean, while I was having a meltdown."

"Yeah, that. Got the impression the cops liked the idea that I was the intended target."

"And you…"

"Thought I'd better know if there's anything extra going on with the Don, considering."

"Extra?"

"Mob war, disputes, anything like that." He popped the top on the Caesar salad. "Anyhow, based on everything I know about these folks, the Don probably thinks you got caught in the crossfire and he's letting you know he's sorry and it won't happen again."

"Crossfire of what?"

"That's the question. It could be something as simple as Lis's drug dealer being upset about losing a good customer…but only an expert knows what's really going on with these folks. There are just too many layers of grudges and disputes, new and old."

"Hence your friend."

"Hence. He texted me that he'll call this evening, so I should know more soon."

"We should probably just eat dinner now, then."

For a moment, he studied the trays on the counter. "Can't say no to DiStefano's."

"And Ersalesi's." I tapped the box. "I'm hoping for cannoli."

"Keep a good thought."

We looked at each other.

This was the part where I might have batted back with a lightly smutty double-entendre. But it didn't feel right yet. Not sure why.

Dinner was every bit as magnificent as you'd expect, and there were indeed cannoli in the Ersalesi's box. We all ate more than we should have and headed into our evening happily well-fed and more relaxed than we should have been.

Especially since it was thanks to Don Nunzio.

Michael was in the living room playing video games with Daniel, and I was cleaning up when my phone buzzed. Unfamiliar number but no spam flag.

Time to dive back into my other major problem.

No pun intended, trust me.

"Grace Adair."

"Well, you sound almost normal." Professor Munroe's tone was cool. "How are you feeling?"

"Still light-sensitive and still very tired, but my brain seems to be working."

"Excellent. Any theories about your mishap?"

I let the question hang for a moment. Surely, she would not have asked if the sisters had had anything to do with it.

"Well," I said finally, "since it was my husband's car, police seem to think it may be related to a case of his."

"That would be a good working hypothesis."

"Or, possibly a shared case. He took the case, but I successfully handled it."

"Hm?"

"Getting a young lady who did something stupid because of a drug problem out of criminal court and into drug court and rehab."

"Doing the Lord's work, perhaps."

"Sure felt like it," I agreed. "But her dealer may not have seen it that way."

"Reasonable theory for the police."

"Well, there's more."

"Oh?" Her voice went up a bit.

"The young lady is the niece of Nunzio Imperiale."

"*That* Nunzio Imperiale?"

"As far as I know, there's only one that matters."

"True. So there may be a larger issue here."

"Exactly," I said. "Michael has a friend in the federal apparatus who is gathering information."

"Good. Keep me apprised."

"Of course."

I waited.

"Now, about the other matter. We are now just a few days from the wedding, and as far as I know, there's no resolution."

"I've started working on a plan, but I haven't been able to complete it."

"I know you've been sidelined, Grace, but you need to act now. You need to settle this."

Somehow, I didn't think she'd accept my calling Al—and Vince's machine—with a piece of my mind as settling anything. "I know. I'll make significant progress tomorrow."

"I certainly hope so." She took a breath, and I could almost hear her thinking. "Look, Grace, the Mothers are very glad that you're all right. I've told you before, you're very valuable to us. I'm sorry that the timing on this is so difficult, but if it's not addressed before the wedding, the options become far less pleasant."

"I know." And so did Madge.

"All right, then. Do your best, and we'll talk tomorrow."

"Thank you."

"Get a good night's sleep. That will help."

Somehow, I doubted it.

Back in the living room, the fellas were having a wonderful time playing some kind of racing game. Even more fun because Daniel was clearly kicking Michael's backside…and taking unholy glee in it.

The rest of the evening was as quiet and normal as could be. Well, except for Daniel very carefully kissing every single scratch and bruise on my face at bedtime, "to make it better."

After he was down, I closed the door and folded into Michael's arms for the hug I'd been needing for hours. I burrowed into his shoulder, my tears soaking into the soft fleece of his house sweatshirt. Not sobbing—just quietly leaking a little.

Of course, that's when his phone buzzed.

"I've got to take this, Tweety," he said.

"I know. I'm fine. Going to bed with a book."

"Good idea."

It took all the energy I had left to change into a sleepshirt and brush my teeth—the vibrating brush was not fun with the concussion. Despite a fair slew of things that should have kept me awake, as soon as I got settled under the covers, I dozed right off.

Could have been minutes, could have been hours later when Michael climbed into bed beside me. I woke to him spooning in, burying his face in my hair.

"Hey," I said.

"You weren't supposed to wake up."

"Like I wouldn't."

"Just needed to hold you, after...everything."

I burrowed into his arms, enjoying the warmth and connection. So good to be in my own bed with my man after everything. Comforting.

And more.

After a couple of breaths, I turned to him.

"Yeah?" he asked.

"Oh, yeah." I kissed him.

He tensed a bit. "I don't want to hurt you..."

"Remember that old Marvin Gaye song?"

"'What's Going On?'"

"'Sexual Healing.'" I slid my hands up his back under the T-shirt, feeling the smooth muscles flex as he pulled me closer. More than anything, right now, I needed him, needed us. Needed the love and magic and fire between us to burn away all the fear and stress of the last few days.

He laughed, almost like normal, and moved to kiss a favorite—unbruised—spot under my ear. "Works for me..."

CHAPTER TWENTY-SIX
ONE MYSTERY SOLVED

Tuesday morning, I woke up early, still spooned in Michael's arms. Since I felt pretty darn good, I decided to go downstairs and attempt some exercise.

The basement lights seemed a little too bright, and I silently thanked our electrician for installing dimmer switches. Sure, I was going to move, but bending my head down for yoga sounded like a truly impossible idea. A little walking on the tread seemed doable.

I started it up and asked Violet the Smart Speaker to play some nice peppy pop music. (Yes, starting with Britney Spears—you got a problem with that?), beginning slowly and picking up speed as I moved. By the end of the first song, I didn't feel awful.

By the end of the second, I was walking at my normal speed, and starting to sweat, beginning to feel warm and smooth and mobile again. And strong. Like I hadn't felt since I saw the big black SUV behind me four—just four?—days ago.

"I'm back, baby!"

Only as I heard it in the quiet room did I feel a little silly.

Not sorry, though.

I wasn't completely back, but I was at least moving in the right direction again.

Taylor Swift finished her song on a triumphant note, and Violet switched to a bright and feisty song by Pink that I really like, so I kept going.

Just let myself enjoy the music and the movement for a few minutes.

Escape from all the madness for a while. I already knew it was going to be a day.

By the time Michael wandered into the kitchen, I'd made coffee and popped bacon in the microwave to go with the toaster waffles—of course, with an extra slice for Scotchie—and packed Daniel's lunch.

"She's back," he said, coming up behind me as I filled his mug, nuzzling my neck.

"I am indeed." I turned to kiss him, and he blinked. "It's the face, isn't it?"

"Let's just say we should leave the lights off for a while. Bruises are definitely not a turn-on."

"That's not a bad thing," I said. "Glad you could get past it."

"Worth it." Sheepish smile. "I didn't…you're…"

"Actually feeling pretty good," I said. "Time to get off the couch for a while."

"Not too long, huh?" He gave me a sharp look. "You're still recovering."

"I know, but I need to move a little."

"Okay, so take Scotchie for his walk after Daniel and I leave. That'll be more than enough for now. Don't forget, the rental people are bringing you your car today."

"You mean, your car. I get mine back."

"Yeah. And I get to start shopping for a new one."

"Everybody wins. I'll be thrilled to have wheels again."

"And I'm thrilled to have you sounding like you again." He planted a careful kiss on my uninjured cheek and headed for the shower.

After everyone was fed, dressed, and packed, I waved the boys off, giving Michael an eye roll after his third reminder to bring my phone and stay close to home.

The walk was really a good idea—it was time for me to get out of the house. And I had a good day for it, the second or third day of our January thaw.

Scotchie sniffed and barked at the bushes by the house when we headed out, as he'd been doing, but I managed to drag him out for a turn around the block. Even though the cut on my leg was starting to hurt, it was good to be out in the fresh air. Since it was a cloudy day, I didn't have the horrible light sensitivity I'd had when Michael brought me home, so it all felt really good.

My giant companion seemed pretty happy too, loping along and sniffing at fire hydrants, menacing passing squirrels, and practically dancing at the end of the leash.

And then we got back to the house.

Scotchie ran up to one of the bushes and started barking like he had before. Pointing like he was alerting on something.

"Okay, fella." I patted him and tried to calm him. He'd never had a run-in with a raccoon like some of the other neighborhood dogs, but anything was possible.

I bent down, following his gaze, and two bright yellow-green eyes met mine.

Cat eyes.

"Back off, big guy," I said, patting Scotchie. "Who do we have here?"

My new friend let out a surprisingly loud and determined howl and moved a bit closer. I could see it wasn't a tiny kitten, but it wasn't full-grown either. In the dim light under the bush, I got a sense of black-and-orange patches. A tortie.

Tortoiseshell cats are special. I couldn't remember why—not that it mattered.

It needed help, and that was enough for me.

"Okay, kiddo." I held out a hand, and the creature sniffed at it, then rubbed against my fingers. "Can you stay here for a moment while I get this guy settled?"

The cat didn't look like it was going to bolt.

I bundled Scotchie inside, grabbed a pouch of the tuna Michael keeps for lunches on the go, and an old plastic container. The kitty was still visible in the bushes.

"Come here, sweetie. Let's get you something to eat."

When I put the tuna into the container, it came right over to me. Poor thing dove right in like it hadn't eaten in days.

Considering Scotchie had alerted on the bushes yesterday, it was possible that it hadn't. Might have been hiding just outside our house, getting a little warmth from the basement window well, and some water from melting snow, for at least a day or two.

"It's okay, sweetie," I said in my best soothing tone. "You're safe with us."

The cat looked up at the sound of my voice and held my gaze. Decided it was okay to trust me for the moment and returned to the food. I watched as it ate, more slowly now. Its fur was sleek, and it looked healthy, so I didn't think it had been living outside for too long. Probably not a feral.

Runaway pet?

No collar.

It could possibly have lost it, but we'd probably know by now if someone in our neighborhood was missing a cat. My guess was somebody had just dumped it. There are still people who will. Well, I'm not sure it's right to call them people. No human worthy of the name would abandon a vulnerable creature.

Somebody had to help this poor animal. And that somebody was me.

I wouldn't have a car to take it to the vet—or anywhere else—for hours, and all my friends were busy. I couldn't leave the little creature outside. What to do?

I'd recently run across somebody who helped feral cats…but who?

As I racked my battered brain, the kitty looked up from the tuna and walked over to me, sat down on my foot and started purring.

The cat knew, even if I couldn't admit it quite yet.

How could I do anything other than take in such a vulnerable creature?

Vulnerable creature.

Ethan Storey worked with ferals.

His phone number was in my call history from the texts.

I scratched the kitty behind the ears with one hand while I tapped and dialed with the other. Probably not the safest and smartest thing, but it would have taken a lot more steel than I had to resist.

Storey picked right up.

"Mrs. Adair?"

"Yeah…this is kind of weird, but I wonder if you can help me."

"Okay…"

"You work with feral cats, right?"

"Yeah."

"I found a cat at my house, and I need somebody to make sure it's okay."

"You want to keep it, don't you?"

"Oh, yeah." There. I said it. "Do you know somebody…"

"Our vet will come to your house."

It hung between us for a moment as I hesitated.

"You don't really want me to know your address, do you?"

"I—"

"I wouldn't give it out if I were you, Mrs. Adair, not with everything else going on." Storey let out a rueful sigh. "I'll call our vet, and she'll call you from the road."

"Thank you."

"Thank you…and good luck."

As I hit End, the tortie cat's eyes fixed on me.

I might just need that luck.

It only took a few minutes for the vet to call me, promising to be there within the hour.

While I waited, I lured the cat into the garage, figuring it was safe enough for us both, bringing out more tuna, a second bowl with water, and plugging in the space heater so we'd be decently comfortable.

As we watched and started getting used to each other, I did a little research online on introducing a new pet to a household with an existing animal and child. Looked like all I needed was a green light from the vet, once my new friend had a checkup and shots.

Well…as long as I didn't mind several weeks—to several years—of absolute chaos.

Not like we didn't have that already.

And what better reason than saving a life?

With more than a little help from Ethan Storey. One more good deed to his credit. I thought about our conversation just before the crash, and the glimmer of an idea I'd had then blossomed into an almost decent plan. We might be able to get out of this after all.

I called him back.

"Mrs. Adair? Is everything okay?"

"Absolutely. She's coming to my house. I wanted to thank you and ask you a favor."

"What?"

"I need your help to do something I think will get my clients to back off for good."

"Really?"

"Really." I told him what I needed, and he didn't even hesitate.

"You're sure you trust me with this?" I confirmed.

"Mrs. Adair, I think I'd trust you with a lot more."

"Thanks." I scratched the kitty behind the ears and her purr grew louder. "Look, I can't make you any promises, but I'm hopeful we can settle this."

"Hopeful is good," he said.

Just then, a battered green SUV pulled into my driveway.

"Gotta go," I said. "She's here."

"'Bye. Tell her I said hi."

"Will do."

A small, spare woman in a sensible navy parka, with a bright red cat-print fleece visible underneath, hopped out, bag in hand, and took a moment to study the scene.

"Ms. Adair?" the vet asked as she walked into the open garage, giving me a big warm smile.

"Yes. Thank you for coming, Dr. Vaughan."

"Of course. Ethan's a good guy."

I nodded.

"I'm sure you know the history, but I know the person he is now." She bent down. "And whatever he was, he is a very decent person now."

"I agree," I said, holding her gaze. Her eyes were bright blue, almost like a Siamese cat's, and her long gray hair was in a neat bun. She moved like a young woman, but I suspected she was in her seventies at least.

She set down her bag and slipped on gloves. "Let's see what we have here."

The kitty moved right to her and only let out a small squawk when she scooped her up. "Well, aren't you a nice girl."

"Girl?"

"Girl." She took a perfunctory look at the tail end of the cat and nodded. "Torties are almost always female—it's a genetic thing. This girl seems to be in good shape. Unless I'm missing something, she wasn't born feral. Too well-tended. Looks like somebody just dumped her off not long ago."

"Poor baby."

"People are crumbs, Mrs. Adair. Animals are much better."

"I'm not going to argue that." I petted the cat, and she rubbed her head against my fingers again. I think I read somewhere it's how they scent-mark their people. Fine by me. "So can I keep her?"

"I don't know why not." She felt the cat's shoulder. "No microchip, so she was probably just dumped when somebody couldn't give away the whole litter. It happens."

"Is she safe to be around my family?"

"Other cats?"

"No. A dog—big fella who found her."

"No one immune-compromised?"

"Nope."

"Good answers." She smiled. "I'll check her for ticks, and give her a couple of shots—rabies and feline leukemia vaccs— and then, fine. You're going to ease her in with other people and animals anyhow."

"Yeah. The online experts say to give her a space in one room and let everyone get used to her slowly."

"That's the theory. Let her set her own limits and see how you do." She nodded to Daniel's bike by the wall. "How old is your child?"

"Six. He'll want to be her friend."

"She'll warm to him—she's a young one too. Just take it slow and let her hide when she wants to."

"We can do that."

After carefully going over the sleek fur to be sure no unwanted travelers were with her, the vet pulled syringes out of her bag and motioned to me. "Soothe her down while we take care of this. You can hold her on your lap if you want to."

"Okay." I pulled the kitty to me, and she settled right in, only letting out a tiny, annoyed squeak at the two shots. Afterward, I kept petting her, and she started purring. A strong, muscle-car engine sound that seemed much larger than her fuzzy body.

"Excellent." Dr. Vaughan smiled and pulled forms out of her bag, clicking a pen. "I need to start records so you can give them to your regular vet. Let's see. Domestic shorthair, probably around six months old...how about a name?"

"Oh...um..." I looked down into the big yellow-green eyes, and knew. There was only one possibility. "Nolo."

"Nola? Pretty. A relative?"

"No," I said with a sheepish shrug. "Nolo for *nolo conten-dere*—no contest. I was gone the minute she looked at me."

Dr. Vaughan grinned, suddenly looking like a sprite—or a fairy godmother. "Lawyer?"

"Yeah."

"Perfect, then."

The newly christened Nolo Adair settled into my arms. "I've got a friend up at Loquat's Hardware who'll make a delivery. I've had cats, but never one this young. What does my girl need?"

Another impish smile. "Kitten food, litter box—she's probably trained—cat bed, a few toys to start. Just get the basics...you can spoil her once she knows she's safe."

"Makes sense to me."

Dr. Vaughan started packing her bag.

I stood, bringing the cat with me. Nolo climbed onto my shoulder and settled there, resting her head in the crook of my neck.

"What do I owe you?" I asked.

"Nothing. I do this pro bono, as you lawyers like to say."

"Bad answer. I'm writing a check today—the only question is where to."

Dr. Vaughan and I agreed on an appropriate donation to the ferals group, and she headed on her way after coming inside to pet Scotchie, wishing us all well and giving the cat one more ear scratch. The whole time, Nolo stayed snuggled into my shoulder, occasionally letting out a happy purr.

By then, it was noon, and I was pretty much done. Whatever energy I'd had early in the day was long since gone. After the doc left, I put the tuna and water bowls in a far corner of the kitchen, texted Michael to call before he came home, and collapsed on the couch.

The rental car woman showed up an hour later, dropping off the only car that was available for long-term use: a good-sized olive-green SUV. It looked like a Sherman tank. I filled out the paperwork, drove my friendly car lady back to her office, and went back to the blanket.

Almost two hours later, when Corinna brought Daniel home, they found the three of us there. Me, asleep with Nolo on my chest, and Scotchie draped over the couch protecting us both.

Welcome to the family.

CHAPTER TWENTY-SEVEN
MEET THE FAM

"What is that?"

When Michael walked in the door at about five thirty, Nolo was still sitting on my shoulder, Scotchie was keeping watch, and Daniel was doing his homework while staring at the cat. Not much math was getting done, but kid and kitty were getting used to each other, and that would probably be more valuable in the long run.

While I was getting Nolo settled, and dealing with the car, I hadn't told Michael about the cat, even though I initially thought about it. Ultimately, I decided it would go much better if he just met her. Corinna had simply shot me a quick wave and told me to give her the whole story in the group text later because it was Cherise's dance class day. Then, Brian, Zooey, and Pete were more than happy to make a delivery, to get a glimpse of Nolo.

The knock on the door had been enough to send her diving under a couch cushion, and there she stayed until they left, so all they got was a good view of her flicking orange-and-black-spattered tail. Once the interlopers were gone, Nolo was happy to accept a real meal and investigate the litter box I'd set up for her in a corner of the basement.

Then she returned to me.

And so, Michael's first sight of her was of two bright eyes in a fuzzy little face peering out from the crook of my neck. He moved toward us, and she tensed for a moment, her small needle claws jabbing through my fleece.

Probably keying on me, picking up my concern about Michael's reaction. We'd both been cat people until Scotchie; my gray tabby, Ginsburg, died shortly before our wedding, and Michael's, a white cat with one black paw named Ace, lasted until a few months before Daniel's birth. Each well into their teens, well-tended and dearly mourned.

But now, with our busy and complex lives, I wasn't at all sure how Michael would take a new addition to the family. Probably should have given it more thought, but here we were.

And she was not negotiable.

"Is that…" Michael continued, moving a bit closer to us. Nolo met his gaze, watching his every move. Not afraid or backing off, though—a credit to both of them.

"It's a kitty, Daddy!" proclaimed Daniel.

"Why yes, it is." Michael flicked a nod to Daniel, then held out his hand so Nolo could take a sniff. His dubious expression melted into a smile. "Do I want to know how this happened?"

"Oh, probably." I patted Nolo, reassuring her. "Scotchie found her in the bushes."

"Of course he did. We're keeping her, right?"

"Good answer, Counselor."

Michael reached a couple of fingers out to the cat, and she rubbed her nose against them. "Well, she is a sweetheart, isn't she?"

"She is." I sat up, carefully moving Nolo onto my lap. She squawked, but settled back in, once I stopped moving.

Michael sat down beside me and gave the kitty a tentative ear scratch. She relaxed right into it, apparently deciding she was safe enough with me to enjoy the attention.

"Did you take her to the vet?"

"Vet came to us. Ethan Storey called her for me."

Michael's eyes widened and he stopped scratching. "Who?"

"Yes, him."

The kitty nudged Michael and he started scratching again. "How…"

"His number was in my call history. I called him and he sent the vet from the feral group he works with. She called me from the road, and I gave her my address."

"If he really wanted to find us, he could check property records, you know."

"Yeah, I know."

"Still smart of you. Especially with everything."

The cat started purring, the same outsize noise she'd made before.

"Wow!" Daniel said, putting down his pencil. "She's vibrating."

"What a purr," Michael agreed. "So, do we have everything we need for her?"

"Brian brought over the basics—I'm out of cash and you're going to see a big check to Feral Friends, by the way—and we'll need to make an expedition to the pet store soon."

"Oh, I think we can handle that." He grinned. "Where does she sleep?"

"We're supposed to keep her in her own room for a while until she gets used to us…but honestly, I think we might do better to let her know where she can hide if she needs to and let her go where she likes."

"Makes sense to me." Michael pulled back, and the kitty settled right down into my lap again. "I think she's happy with you."

"I'm just the one who found her. We'll have to watch out for her. We aren't used to having anything small underfoot."

"True. She's a little bigger than a new kitten, but she's going to be everywhere once she gets used to the place."

"Can I pet her, Ma?" Daniel approached, holding a hand out, copying his dad.

"Let her sniff you first, son." Michael showed him the right way, and Nolo accepted a tentative pet, purring a bit louder.

Unlike Jimmy Stewart, the hardware store cat, she seemed genuinely happy for the attention.

Jimmy was a found kitty too, but she seemed to have a lot more attitude.

Of course, who knew what kind of attitude Nolo would have once she was safe, fed, and comfortable. Especially once she realized she'd found a family who would happily grant her every wish.

While Michael's reaction to Nolo was all I could have hoped for, the rest of the evening was a bit more elaborate. First, we had to trade keys and info so Michael could drive the tank in the morning and I could be back in my car. Then back inside— to find Nolo sitting in the window watching for us like the poor lost creature she'd been when she woke up that day.

It wasn't easy heating up a casserole, helping Daniel with his homework, and doing laundry with a cat on my shoulder, but we managed.

She was still sitting on my shoulder when Professor Munroe called, and her purr sounded like a seal of approval when the professor accepted my plan to settle matters, though she wasn't wild about the timing. Still, it wasn't a bad way to end an eventful day.

The best moment came at the end, when Nolo flatly refused to take her spot on a kitty bed in the living room, following me into the bedroom and nesting in the spot between Michael's and my pillows.

I fell asleep to the sound of her purr.

CHAPTER TWENTY-EIGHT
HOT UNDER THE COLLAR

The next morning dawned bright and cold.

I wasn't sure which one bothered me more.

The cold hit me first, when I woke a few minutes before my alarm was supposed to go off and my feet hit the chilly bedroom floor. Nolo jumped down and followed me into the kitchen, purring, whether in anticipation of morning treats or just to remind me she was there and adorable.

Either way worked for her.

Like most cats, Nolo had exactly zero interest in exercise—or cold—and she scampered back to the bedrooms while I went downstairs to the treadmill. Thanks to the cold, it took me most of the walk to feel decent, but I was finally loosened up and humming when I got upstairs.

To take a big bright ray of light in the face.

Before the crash, it would have felt good. Warm winter sunlight is a gift.

Except when it slashes through your skull and makes

your stomach twist. I stepped out of the light, took a couple of breaths, and pulled down the shade on the back door. Nolo reappeared and rubbed against my ankle, whether checking on me or asking for seconds on breakfast, who knew?

By the time Michael and Daniel awakened, I'd settled down enough that I could move, but I sure wasn't going to be back to that nice zen I'd had on the way up. Zen or no zen, I was still glad to get back to some semblance of normal mom life.

Even with breakfast and packing lunch, I had enough time before drop-off to grab a quick shower and throw on a thick purple chenille sweater and black velour leggings, even swipe on a dab of my favorite pink lip balm, mostly for the sweet scent—I wasn't sure I wanted to draw attention to anything about my face.

The good news was, I was driving my car, and Michael had the rented Sherman tank.

Daniel was happy to go to school most days anyway, but he was clearly delighted to have me back on the run, chattering happily and asking me if we'd be getting Cherise and Zooey at pickup today. This early, it was a hard maybe. With Corinna in budget season, and Brian possibly facing a paint emergency at any time, the afternoon could go a bunch of ways.

The first drop-off since the crash should have been a party, but the single-digit temps ruined it. When it's that cold, we go back to the old Covid drug-deal drop, pulling up at the portico and letting the kids run to the staffer holding the door.

Not nearly as much fun.

At least I could catch up with Corinna and Brian later in the group chat.

As I drove out of the traffic circle, I thought about my to-do list for the day and decided to stop over at Loquat's Hardware to get Nolo a collar. Old Man Loquat opened the store when Brian left for drop-off, so I'd definitely get to see the patriarch, and maybe Brian too, if he came straight back.

The store was already open, with several people inside when I opened one of the big old wood-and-glass double doors. It seemed a little heavier than it had the last time I'd been there.

"Here, let me help you with that, Grace."

I recognized the voice: Hot Dad Todd Derevenko.

That's what the moms—and some of the dads—call him. He's one of the best-looking guys in the parent pool: tall, dark, and handsome with the kind of naughty smile that recalls Robert Urich on *Spenser for Hire*. (I grew up watching my uncle Cal's old VHS tapes…had a crush before I even knew what a crush was!)

Todd's a stay-at-home dad with a wife who's an exec in New York, and he's universally acclaimed as a bit of a flirt. Which is fine. It wasn't until a few weeks ago when I found out he was into a lot more than flirting that it became an issue.

Apparently, he and his wife are "open," as the modern term of art goes. I don't get to judge, but I do get to question a guy's judgment when he makes a play for one of the PTA moms in the coffee line at Louisa's like he did in December. We'd left it well, but it was still a little weird.

Even if I'd enjoyed the attention just a tiny bit.

There's nothing wrong with honest, harmless flirting, after all. Appreciating and being appreciated by a fellow attractive person just makes you feel better about yourself when you go home to your partner. It's only a problem if it goes beyond that.

Anyhow, I would definitely not have chosen Hot Dad Todd as the first person to interact with under any circumstances, and certainly not on my first real day back in the world. Events very quickly confirmed my misgivings.

"Thanks," I said, turning toward him.

The wicked little grin faded like I'd slapped him. "Oh, my God, Grace. I heard about the crash, but…"

Great. Just what I needed. "Superficial."

"Um, yeah." He let out a nervous cough, almost in my face. Because not only did I need to be treated like a visiting zombie, I also needed a good load of the current virus.

"I'll be fine," I told him, with more than a little ice in my tone, and stepped off in the direction of pet supplies.

Out of the corner of my eye, I saw Old Man Loquat shaking his head.

I'd definitely enjoy talking to him. But first, a collar for my new family member.

Nolo wasn't tiny enough for a kitten collar, so I started with the "small cat" ones. Like everything else at Loquat's, the selection was more limited and more special than the big box stores. You come to Loquat's because you want products that work and last. Almost nothing here is rock-bottom cheap or disposable. Not that prices aren't reasonable and fair, but they fit the New England philosophy: buy good, reliable things and keep them.

Exactly the kind of place I want to shop, especially in the world we live in.

The small cat collars came in a variety of colors, mostly the standard nylon webbing with a loop for the rabies tag and ID, and a bell. Considering my cat was a variety of colors, I wasn't really sure what to do. Black or orange to match? Purple for contrast? Pink because she's a girl? And then I saw a little glitter. It wasn't blinding enough to trigger my light sensitivity. Just a shimmery black piece with a black metal bell. Perfect and pretty for my new tortie girl.

As I pulled it off the peg, I noticed Hot Dad Todd further down the aisle picking up dog food and casting surreptitious glances at me. It felt stalker-y and weird.

Maybe I was just oversensitive.

Maybe there was still some weirdness because he'd made that play a few weeks ago.

Or maybe something else was going on.

I didn't know what the something else might be.

But just then, my battered brain landed on Ronald Doremus—Cathie Holman's last attacker—reminding me we had no idea what had become of him. Could have just been a coincidence. Lord knew I'd been having odd dreams and screwball random thoughts. Or it might have been something alerting in my subconscious.

What did we know about Ronald Doremus, after all?

Not flipping much.

Wherever he turned up as an adult, *if* he did, he'd have a new name and a new background. And he probably wouldn't look like the booking photo, since he'd been just at that mid-teen stage where people are unformed and could end up looking entirely different.

I didn't honestly think Todd Derevenko was Ronald Doremus. For one thing, he carried himself like a person who'd been attractive for his whole life. It's not something you can learn, and not something you see with people who grew into their looks. Michael, for example, is universally acclaimed as devastating now…but until sometime in his college years, he was a reedy, weird-looking ginger kid, with features that didn't quite fit and an unappealing awkwardness in his stance.

Michael still seems surprised when people react to him as a gorgeous man. It's a chemical thing, a half-second "Who, me?" moment he can't fake. Based on the booking photos, if Doremus had ended up attractive, he'd have the same sort of attitude, not Todd's easy, almost-but-not-quite-arrogant acceptance of his appeal.

So I was probably borrowing trouble—as both Michael's and my Scots grandmothers used to say—about Todd.

Probably.

I wasn't borrowing trouble about Doremus, though. Not even a little. He really could be somewhere just outside the line of my vision, plotting who knows what. Hiding in plain sight. I know something about the dynamic, after all. The person you're not looking at, the person you'd never consider—maybe the person you just casually dismiss and walk past—that's the one you need to worry about.

Ronald Doremus definitely called for further consideration. He might even be stalking Ethan Storey. Al and Vince might not be responsible for all of it.

Well, wasn't that a cheerful thought?

All of these delightful possibilities were swirling in my brain as I made my way to the counter with the collar. Old Man Loquat was still there, holding court as he does for an hour or so each morning and afternoon, despite his great age.

"Gracie!" He grinned. "So good to see you."

His pleasure at seeing me was real, and not even a little diluted by the way I looked. A warm, wonderful embrace of good energy.

I love this man.

"So good to see *you*," I replied. "I know I look a bit rough."

"You look like you've survived something." He met my gaze squarely. "Nothing to be ashamed of. And if anybody gives you any guff about it, you send 'em to me."

"Will do, sir." I smiled.

His eyes narrowed a little. "Your fella's not acting weird about it?"

"Not at all. First time I looked at myself in the mirror, he told me I was still the most beautiful woman he'd ever seen."

"And he meant it. Always meant it when I said that to my wife." Wistful smile as he patted my hand. "You've got a good one, Gracie."

"I sure think so."

He looked down at the collar and nodded. "And what do we have here? A new friend for the big lug?"

"The big lug found her."

"Really?" The old gent's face lit up. "Tell me!"

Since there was no one else in line, I happily gave him the short version, and he absorbed every word with joy.

"Brian brought us the basics yesterday, but she'll need a collar if we're taking her with us to Madge's wedding this weekend. The hotel's small-pet friendly, so why not?"

"Should have a collar anyhow. You never know."

"Absolutely." He rang up the collar and reached for a packet of Sardine Surprise treats. "Here. From Jimmy and me to welcome the new arrival."

"Aww, thank you." I took the items and receipt and stowed them in the deep pocket of my puffer. "You, Brian, and Zooey should come over to have dinner and meet Nolo soon."

"Sounds great. We'll bring the pizza."

"I'll make the spice cake. Been needing an excuse to make Grandma's penuche fudge icing."

"Penuche? I didn't know anyone even made that anymore."

"It's not easy, but it's worth it. Next week, after the wedding, okay?"

"You've got a deal. Looking forward to it."

As I headed for the door, I heard a ruffly noise. Jimmy Stewart was keeping her person's rocking chair warm. I stopped to pet her but got a warning yowl when she smelled Nolo. I shot a quick wave back to Old Man Loquat.

"See you at the wedding if not before!"

"Got that, Gracie!"

"Thanks!"

On the edge of my vision, I saw someone moving up to the counter, but a ray of sunshine slammed right into my face, and my stomach lurched.

As I scrabbled to pull my sunglasses down and regain my balance, I heard Old Man Loquat ask: "How's Jakie?"

I was glad I'd missed a pointless run-in with JakesPop, but it didn't really matter. Mr. Loquat could have been greeting the Dalai Lama for all I cared at that point. What I needed was to get the light out of my eyes and sit down.

Not necessarily in that order.

Sunglasses down, I sat for a few minutes in the car, trying to get myself together. Stuck my head out the open door and took a couple of deep breaths of the cold, cold air. Normally, I'd hate it, but the chill actually helped settle my stomach and wake me up a little.

After a minute or so, I closed the door and folded over the steering wheel of the disturbingly empty car. My eyes were welling up.

Michael didn't have to worry about me thinking I was a hundred percent.

I wasn't even on the chart yet.

CHAPTER TWENTY-NINE
BAD BOYS, WHAT YOU GONNA DO?

If I'd been hoping for a restful morning with my new friend, that hope evaporated within about five minutes after I got home from the hardware store.

I'd just clasped the collar around Nolo's neck and given her one of Jimmy's favorite treats as a reward for her compliance when I saw a huge copper and ivory shape pull into the driveway.

Al and Vince, in the Bonneville.

Well, at least I got to look at the car.

It really was a treasure. A rare and beloved vintage car that had been a key piece of evidence in a criminal case late last year, it was Vince's gift to himself. As I understood it, he'd been saving a little bit here and a little bit there for fifty years in the hope that he'd someday find just the right ride. When the car owner needed to make a quick sale for his murder defense, Vince happened to hear about it, and he was more than happy to pay a fair, if not exorbitant, price.

Yes, it took a certain amount of inside information sharing to make it happen, but everybody—with the possible exception of the murderer, who'd taken a plea for twenty-to-life—was glad to see the car with somebody who would cherish it.

Vince should have garaged the car for the winter, but because it was a new acquisition, he'd been sneaking it out on dry days. Which is why Ethan Storey had seen our superannuated bad boys cruising around. And why they were in the Bonneville today, instead of Al's sensible dark-green SUV, or Vince's old, but not vintage, beige sedan.

"Well, Nolo, hope you want to make new friends," I said, walking to the door with the cat snuggled into my shoulder.

Al had a big bouquet in hand, assorted flowers in spring pastels that might as well have had a sign on them reading Peace Offering. Vince was carrying a small bakery box with Ersalesi's distinctive red-and-blue string.

I went to the storm door and waved.

Nolo dug in as I opened it, but didn't move.

"Who's this?" Al asked.

"What a pretty little girl," Vince added.

Both took a good look at the cat without invading her space. Nolo gave them a glance and a sniff, but didn't move off my shoulder. This spoke well of everyone.

"Scotchie found her in the bushes yesterday. She's staying."

"Well, I should hope so." Al nodded.

"Does she have a name yet?" Vince asked.

"Nolo."

Vince got it immediately and beamed. Al took a second but then grinned too.

"No contest, huh?" Vince asked.

"Not a bit."

They smiled at the cat like the adorable oldsters they wanted people to think they were.

I, however, knew the truth—and they knew I knew.

"Here." Al held out the bouquet. "Flowers for the ladies."

I took it, and the cat sniffed with me.

She sneezed and jumped down off my shoulder, swaggering away the way cats do when they're trying to be cool.

"It's a cat." Vince chuckled and held out the box. "Cannoli."

"Peace offerings are nice," I said, then narrowed my eyes. "They are not, however, a substitute for obeying your conditions of release."

"Oh, hell, Grace." Al sat down on the couch.

"We're just trying to—" Vince began.

"Ruin your own lives in the hopes of gaining some kind of vengeance?" I glared at them both. "Come on."

"That kid doesn't deserve to be running around free," growled Al.

"The judicial system has decided he's no longer a threat to the community," I reminded them. "And I've talked to him. He's well aware of the harm he caused and has spent the last decade and a half trying to do good. Works with ex-cons, helps feed the hungry, volunteers with feral cats, for heaven's sake."

"C'mon, Grace, you're not buying that crap." Vince stared at me.

"Not in every case. A whole lot of people get a whole lot less prison time than they deserve. But this guy knows his debt, and he's tried to pay it. You're just going to ruin your own lives."

Both scowled at me.

"He told me what he did that night," I continued. "Actually, what he didn't do."

"Yeah, and?" Al snarled.

"And maybe you should focus on pursuing people who deserve it. There are plenty of them."

"Not ones who attacked Cathie Holman," Vince said.

And the light dawned.

"You're going after Ethan because he's the only one left you can find."

They glared at me.

"So you two don't know where Ronald Doremus is, either."

"How would I?" Al asked.

Vince just shook his head.

"No records? No backdoor whispers?"

"I got nothin'." Vince sighed. "Not one damn thing."

"And we've tried," Al said. "Online searches, even had a friend on the Feds rummage around for me."

"No sign of him?"

"Nope." Vince rubbed his face with his hands. "He disappeared from the records after he finished his sentence in juvie."

"Juvie." Al spat the word as if it tasted bad. Which it probably did.

"As I understand it," I began carefully, "he actually deserved far more than he got."

"Damn right he did." Al shook his head. "A couple of months older, and we'd have gotten him for attempted murder."

"Boss wouldn't go for attempted murder for Storey because he cooperated," Vince growled. "Said it would send a bad message to future witnesses."

"Back to Doremus for a minute," I said. "He drops off the map after the sentence."

"Yeah." Al gave me a glance. "Do you have any coffee?"

"I'll make some. Sounds like I'm going to need it." I stood and put myself right into the ray of light coming through the blinds. Ow.

"Oh, jeez, Grace." Vince was up first.

"You okay?" Al jumped up too, both of them surrounding me and awkwardly reaching for me, trying to be supportive but not weird.

"Light sensitivity," I said, taking a breath to quiet my stomach. "Doc says it'll go away with time. If one of you can close the blinds, it'll help."

"You don't need to make coffee," Vince began.

"Yeah, actually I do," I assured him. "The caffeine might help."

Al hovered at my elbow as I walked to the kitchen.

"Go sit and see if the cat will let you pet her," I said. "I'm fine."

By the time I got the pot going and took a few deep breaths to calm the nausea, the cat had returned to the living room and taken up a spot on the coffee table, where she was studying Al and Vince, and the two were carefully holding out their hands for a sniff.

"What a lovely cat," Vince said. "Not quite as wonderful as my little Baci, but adorable."

"Show her the pic," Al urged. "He's got one of Baci with the Bonneville keys."

"You should start taking pics of this girl," Vince said. "You could put them online."

"Oh, hell no."

Nolo stalked away from the guys and nudged my hand, mewing. I picked her up and she climbed right back to her usual spot on my shoulder.

"All right," I said, sitting back down with the cat. "It's going to be a couple minutes for the coffee."

"That's fine," Vince said. "You can tell us the whole story of how you found her."

"Well, first, you need to know who sent the vet to the house," I said, petting Nolo as she started to purr, a softer sound than the one she made when she was alone with me, but still a big announcement that she was feeling happy and safe.

"You got a house call?" Al asked.

"Yep. Someone who works with ferals had a friend who was willing to come over."

"Someone?" Vince's eyes narrowed a bit.

Al moved his gaze from the cat's face to mine.

"Ethan Storey, actually. He knew the vet and called her for me."

A small brow flick from Al, a twist of the mouth from Vince.

"Your point is?" Al asked.

"My point is, while the vet was working on Miss Nolo here, she also gave me a little background on the person Ethan Storey is today."

Vince let out a derisive snort. "Rehabilitated?"

"I wouldn't use that word, and I doubt he would either. But he's not the guy who crouched in the bushes that night."

"And that's supposed to make it all right?" Al asked.

"It might give you a way to move forward without getting stuck on taking vengeance. A way to find a little mercy for him."

Another snort from Vince.

"And a way to keep yourselves out of trouble." I gave them both as hard a look as I could manage with a scrambled brain and bruised face. "Lieutenant Luciano was willing to give you a break last time. If it gets back to her desk, it's not going to be pretty."

"Carla's a good lady," Al said. "I trained her, you know. Too bad about her wife."

"Wife?" Vince's tone suggested he might not be entirely comfortable with the idea of good ladies having wives.

"First woman firefighter to die in the line in New Haven. You remember."

"Yeah, I do now." Vince nodded, the uncertain tone evaporating at the fact of a widowed member of the service. "She's raising a little girl, right?"

"Tween, actually," I said. "And I agree, she's a good lady. But she won't be able to give you any room if you push this. Both of you know that."

Little grumbly noises that wouldn't have been out of place on the cat.

The coffeepot beeped.

Vince pointed to the box. "We brought cannoli."

Convenient change of topic.

But one I was willing to take. With assurances.

"All right." I stood, and Nolo hopped back down to the table. "We're all clear here, right? No more out-of-line behavior?"

"I'm busy with wedding planning," Al said.

"Got a trial coming up," Vince said.

It wasn't a promise, but it was as good as I was probably going to get from them. And it would do for now.

Not that I thought for a minute things were settled for good.

CHAPTER THIRTY
ON THE BOOKS

D aniel got his wish. With Corinna's budget meeting running long, and Brian in the middle of a donnybrook over grout colors, I was the designated hitter for pickup. And glad to repay a little of the help I'd gotten lately.

While it was still bitterly cold, I did get out of the vehicle, exchange the word of the day ("tortie" in honor of Nolo), and herd the kids to their ride. With Daniel leading the way, they sprinted across the lot, then swarmed into the back seat, giggling at being back together in their usual spot.

"Where are we going?"

"Library," I said. Daniel and I had planned a visit today anyhow because we were both low on reading material, and Corinna's situation just made it that much easier. By the time everyone was supplied with books, the budget meeting would probably be over, and Brian would be out from under the grout situation.

Alcott has one of the best libraries in New Haven County, with a sizeable adult section, packed with bestsellers and sleeper surprises, and a warm and welcoming children's room deliberately designed to foster young readers. Corinna and her recently retired boss, Moira, spent a lot of time creating an amazing environment for book people of all ages.

The minute the automatic doors open, there's a noticeable waft of new-book scent, with an undertone of old paper, plus hints of good coffee, greenery from the plants, and a trace of vanilla from the open—but never lit—candle on the charge desk. It's like a voice saying: "We read here, and you're welcome to join us."

The kids took off ahead of me, not-quite-running but moving very quickly to get to their own sanctuary.

"Grace?"

I turned at the sound of my name. Moira was standing at the book drop, in jeans and a bright plaid fleece under a heavy black down coat, looking happier and more relaxed than I'd ever seen her. Her cheery smile faded as she got a look at my face.

"Wow. I'd like to see the other guy."

The joke was getting very, very old, but Moira had no way to know. And it was so good to see her. "So would I. Some fool ran me off the road into the water."

"Holy hell." She put a hand on my arm. "You're okay?"

"Healing nicely."

"What happened? Do they know…"

"Hard to be sure—I was in Michael's car when it happened."

"Yikes. Accident, I hope?"

"Unclear right now."

"Somebody could be after one of you?"

"Maybe." I shrugged. "Police are kind of going on the assumption that it might be the drug dealer of a woman we're defending,"

"Drug dealer?" Moira blinked. "That's not cool."

"No, but at least it's straightforward. They're mad I got one of their cash cows into drug court. Don't have to go chasing down every current and former client from the last forever."

"True," Moira agreed. "But some of our KidsRead families have had run-ins with the crews in New Haven, and those boys are pretty rough."

"Cheer me up some more, why don't you." I took a breath. "Honestly, I'd be pretty surprised if she had a seriously hardcore dealer—she was a high school athlete who spiraled after an injury."

"Ugh."

"Yeah. Good kid, decent family, just got sucked into the whole mess. I actually think she has a shot."

"Well, that's good to hear. But the cops could be right if your girl was buying from the wrong guys. Especially since you got her into drug court. They might be trying to make an example."

"Discourage anyone else from getting help and getting out?"

"Exactly. Remember, that world's very basic. Money and respect. That's about it."

"And getting a customer out through drug court is a smack in both places."

"Yep. The good news is, these guys don't do long vendettas like the mob boys."

"Because they usually kill their victims outright?"

"Nah. Most of 'em use too much of their own product to hold a grudge for long. They'll also figure they made their point. Unless you manage to get crosswise with them again somehow."

"Well, I could if I take another drug court case."

"This is going to sound horrible. Insensitive, classist, all kinds of wrong, okay?"

"Okay."

"But you know it's me saying it, and that I don't see anyone as disposable—or make judgments based on anything other than character."

"Right."

"Okay then. Just stay away from drug court for a few months, and your enemies will be dead, one way or another."

I remembered my days as a prosecutor, and the drug cases that fell apart on a regular basis. "You're probably right."

"I don't want to be. But on the other hand, anybody who's coming for you deserves all kinds of bad things to happen to them."

"Well…"

"I'm sure Michael feels the same way."

"Probably just as well he's been busy dealing with the car and all the other practical stuff." I shrugged. "Anyhow, it's so good to see you."

"It is, as they say, good to be seen. I knew I'd love working at KidsRead, but I didn't know how much I'd love it."

"Well, you always say, it's often the first hand up," I reminded her. KidsRead brings free books to children at churches, shelters, food banks, community centers, and just about any other place you can name. They also work with most of the other local nonprofits and put their clients in touch with them. Moira and her colleagues actually have a terrific track record of helping people because almost nobody will turn down a free book for their child—and it often ends up being a great opener for other services.

"True. And I'm so glad I took retirement so I can do this."

"Is your mom doing okay?" I asked. Her mother was in memory care, paid for by her father's mesothelioma settlement.

"Pretty much. We're lucky—she's one of the happy ones. She doesn't always know me, but she seems pretty comfortable. You know, it doesn't always go that way."

"Yeah." I did. My late grandmother had spent much of her last year cowering in fear from unseen demons. Not a thought I needed right now. "So it sounds like it all worked out."

"Sure did." She grinned. "See you at Madge's wedding this weekend?"

"Darn right." I motioned to my face. "I'm hoping to heal enough to cover this."

"Keep hoping." She winced at herself. "Sorry. Makeup artists can do miracles."

"She's already had her miracle for the month." Corinna was walking up to us, a tiny furrow at her brow indicating she'd had more than enough of the budget process for the day.

"Probably true. But I can still pray for a good cover stick, can't I?"

She took a look at me in the soft, warm light of the library. "You're going to need it."

"Great." I sighed.

"Sorry." Moira and Corinna said in unintended unison.

"No, no. Better to know."

"Love to stay and chat," Moira said, glancing at the giant pocket watch clock on the wall, "but I've got a four p.m. appointment with a family who literally just got off the bus."

"Go," I said.

"Yeah," Corinna added. "And tell them we're glad they're here too."

"Will do. See you at the wedding." Moira gave Corinna an enthusiastic hug, and me a careful one, and then practically skipped away.

"Makes retirement look good, doesn't she?" I asked.

"Does she ever."

"How go the budget wars?"

"Not so bad. It's just been a day. One thing after another. Book club decided they want a dozen copies of that new movie star memoir and I had to horse-trade to get them. Supplier lost our new shipment somewhere in New Jersey. JakesPop felt the need to interrogate me about why the Winter Reading Fest includes a couple books on climate change. And now the budget meeting."

"JakesPop isn't into climate change?" I asked.

"I think he was just being a pain." She shrugged. "Oh, and by the way, he says hi and get well soon."

"He does?"

"Yeah, apparently he was pretty concerned for you."

"Afraid he'll have to do more work at Parent Days."

"Lose no money on that bet. Thanks for getting Cherise."

"Thank you for everything over the last few days. You guys have saved me."

"That's what friends are for."

"Don't sing it," I warned.

"How 'bout I do?"

Brian walked in, looking almost as beleaguered as Corinna had.

"What's yours?" Corinna asked.

"Grout." He threw his hands in the air.

Okay, I'll take the hit. "I know I'm going to regret asking this, but how can you have drama over grout?"

"I'm calling it 'Fifty Shades of Grout.'"

We laughed, exactly as he'd wanted.

"You think grout can be white or gray, right?"

"Pretty much." Corinna said.

"Oh, no. There are custom color blends. Elsa Armitage wants eggshell to complement her beige tile. Not almond or cream, but *eggshell*. She's still over at the store with her contractor. I handed them off to my great-uncle. I couldn't take any more."

"No wonder," I patted his arm. "Well, you're safe here."

"At least for the moment."

We spent a few happy minutes catching up on the stuff that really mattered: kids, pets, dinner. Nothing serious or weird or ugly.

After a few minutes, a ping from Corinna's phone broke the spell, and we reluctantly moved to scoop up our kids and get back to real life, with promises of a big multi-family dinner some night next week.

Little did I know how much non-grout drama I'd have to survive to get there.

CHAPTER THIRTY-ONE
FROM ANOTHER ANGLE

For the rest of Wednesday and into Thursday morning, the only drama was Scotchie and Nolo's first difference of opinion. At dinnertime, the dog made the mistake of sniffing at the cat's food bowl, and she responded as any reasonable feline would: with a hiss and a swipe.

Scotchie, with little experience of these strange small creatures, was absolutely terrified. He squealed and ran off, which then scared Nolo. They proceeded to spend the evening slinking around the house, trying to avoid each other. Finally, at some point in the night, Scotchie wandered into our bedroom, probably forgetting Nolo's new spot between Michael and me.

Whatever happened, they settled it without bloodshed, because I woke to Scotchie sleeping at the foot of the bed, with Nolo beside him, one paw resting on his flank. Friends again.

If we could only settle the rest of our issues so smoothly.

After drop-off, real and serious trouble blasted back with a vengeance.

My phone buzzed as I got back into the car, with a text from Ethan Storey: "I'm sorry, Mrs. Adair, but they're following me again. It's not the Bonneville, but an SUV. Please tell them to stop."

Oh, you bet I will.

I took a couple of breaths to calm my fury, then called back. "Mr. Storey, I promise you, this will stop."

"Thank you. I haven't seen the Bonneville since you had a word with them, but I've seen this dark SUV at least twice in the last few days."

"Dark? What kind of dark?" I asked. "And how big?"

"One of the big guys. Not new, though. I think black."

I wondered. Al's Jeep was actually a medium-size model, but it looked huge to me, since I drive a smallish sedan. Al's Jeep was also a deep forest green color. And Vince's non-Bonneville car was one of the last Buick sedans. Sand beige. "Could it have been dark green?"

"It was a cloudy day. I'm really not sure."

I sighed. "There's at least a possibility it wasn't Al and Vince."

"You mean somebody else is after me?"

"I'd sure like to think not. Especially since I had a run-in with a big dark SUV not long ago."

"Who would want both of us?"

"Good question," I said. I could think of a couple of people we had in common…but Dr. Vaughan probably wasn't running people off the road. And she didn't even know me until after my little swim—so probably had no reason to hate me.

"What the hell is going on?" Sheepish pause. "Sorry, Mrs. Adair."

"I've heard the word." Even sent some deserving men there. "Look, I don't know what is happening here. What I do know is you need to look out for yourself. I have no reason to think anyone means you harm. My clients, whatever their flaws, would never physically attack you. But if it's not my clients…"

"It could be anything. Even the person who ran you off the road."

"Precisely. So please, please, be careful."

"Um, yeah." Deep breath, long sigh. "I will."

"It's the best I've got," I said. "I think we're close to some progress with my clients, so at least one thing should be off the map soon."

"And if it's all there is..."

"We're all good."

"But if not?"

"Not." I took a breath. "Look, once the matter with my clients is settled, I may be able to bring in some other help. Or at least get a sympathetic ear from one of my police contacts."

"I doubt the cops have much sympathy for me."

"Well, somebody had enough sympathy for you to get Vince and Al arrested, so..."

"Fair point." He was quiet for a moment, and I heard his breath down the line. Tense. "Look, I'm working so hard to be a good person and..."

"You are a good person," I said. "Now."

"But the kid I was will never go away."

"Some people only see him. Dr. Vaughan doesn't...and neither do I."

"Oh."

"Now please, just be careful and good to yourself for a bit. Before you know it, you'll be watching the big game and I'll be dancing at a wedding."

"I don't like football. Don't like real-life violence."

No argument from me. I disappear when Michael and Daniel watch the Jets. "Then you'll be watching the Classic Channel's James Bond marathon, but you get the idea."

"Yeah, I do. Always liked Sean Connery."

"Al is about to become the step-pet-parent to a cat by that name."

"Nice."

"We think so."

"Mrs. Adair?"

"Yeah?"

"What did you name your new cat?"

"Nolo, for—"

"*Nolo contendere.* No contest."

"Yep. She had me the minute I saw her."

"Good for you. And her."

"Oh, I sure think so." I took a breath and pulled myself into my most serious lawyer calm. "Now, try to relax. Remember, I asked your help with that little matter? This is going to work."

"Promise?"

"A good lawyer never makes a promise on their client's behalf to another interested party. So let's just say you've helped me take a direction that should lead to a good resolution."

"Your lips to God's ears."

I'd be happy with a somewhat lower power, actually.

CHAPTER THIRTY-TWO
BEAUTY—AND CRIMESTOPPERS—TIPS

By midday, I'd nailed down the last details of my plan and left messages for Al and Vince ordering them to behave—and get back to me. I was dozing after plowing through emails when Carla Luciano called. My first thought when I saw the ID was trouble on the Vince and/or Al front, and I picked up with a cautious tone.

"Grace Adair."

"Hey, Grace. Carla. Passing through on my way back to the office from this morning training thing up in Hartford. If you've got a minute, I can bring you that aloe stuff I used for the glass frag."

"Thanks. That's so kind of you. I'll start the coffee...and I have plenty of baked goods."

"Bet you do." A chuckle. "Everyone's been bringing you stuff, right?"

"Oh, yeah."

"Well, this will actually be helpful—I hope. Give me the address, and I'll see you in about twenty minutes."

"GPS?" I asked.

"Yeah. If it's not in New Haven proper, I rely on the little voice. Makes my life a lot easier."

"Makes sense to me."

I told her my address and went to start the coffee. By the time she pulled up in a very sensible, American-made sedan that looked like an unmarked—and probably was—I'd arranged the hot coffee, two mugs, and a plate of Ersalesi's cannoli on the table.

Nolo had retaken her spot on my shoulder, and didn't move when I went to the door and welcomed our latest visitor.

"Emotional support animal?" she asked, meeting Nolo's curious gaze.

"Found stray. Turned up in the bushes two days ago."

"Just before the cold snap. Sounds like it was good timing for both of you."

"Definitely. Her name's Nolo."

"As in *nolo contendere*? Fun." She held out a jar, taking a closer look at my face. "Yeah, you're going to be glad for this."

"Works?"

"Damn near magic. I'm sorry. I should have brought it over sooner—those cuts don't look deep enough to scar, but you could have healed faster. And with the wedding coming up…"

"I'm putting my faith in concealer." I motioned to the couch.

"Good idea. Don't mess with the funny colored ones, though. I tried green and ended up looking like the Wicked Witch's Italian sister." She shrugged off her coat, a very simple but very good black wool, revealing a pinstriped suit and wine-colored oxford, and sat. Nolo hopped off my shoulder and headed for the coat.

"Do you mind?" I asked.

"Nah." Carla smiled at the cat as she nested into the coat. "She can probably see Teddy's hair. He's a tuxie and somehow manages to shed only white hairs on black."

"They seem to be good at custom shedding. Coffee?"

"Black."

"There's any other way?"

"Not on duty, for sure."

"Woman after my own heart." I poured two mugs and handed her one.

She took a careful sip, and then a larger one. "Ah, you know for coffee."

"Can't not, in New Haven County."

"Oh, you can. You wouldn't believe the stuff people drink. Back when I was in the bag, folks would sometimes offer us coffee at big scenes, and we had to be nice. I don't miss that."

"I bet." I held out the plate. "Cannoli? They're Ersalesi's."

"We both know I shouldn't, and we both know I'm going to." She took one with a grin.

"Yeah. Me too." I picked up my own. "Would you have rather I offered you the antioxidant healing bundt cake?"

"Holy hell no. What even *is* that?"

"Something from some influencer. The PTA president brought it to me. Along with her complaints that we didn't tell her about Eric Egan's past."

"Ah, because of course, lawyers are omniscient."

"Aren't we?"

Carla laughed and took a generous bite of cannoli.

So did I.

No need to talk for a moment, while we appreciated the perfect balance of crisp shell, rich cannoli cream, and tasty bits of chocolate and candied orange peel.

"Ersalesi's is a national treasure," she said finally.

"True that." I put down my pastry.

"Your PTA lady upset because her kids were around Egan?"

"Not really. More wounded pride because she said nice things about him at a parent meeting after."

"Probably the only person who will." Carla shook her head. "Nobody's even claimed the body."

"Really? Sad."

"Yeah. But I'd hate to think of his mom having to know what he was."

We were both quiet for a moment, thinking like mothers rather than police or lawyers.

I owed her some honesty. "You know this by now, I found out Egan was bad news. And I very quietly put the word out to folks to keep their kids away from him."

"Confidentiality concerns?"

"Exactly. But I had an ethical duty of care, so…"

"So you put out just enough."

"But not so much that I could get sued."

"Stand-up lady." She smiled. "Just so you know, I'm not one of those cops who hate lawyers. I almost became one."

"Really."

"Really. I was waitressing for a year to raise money for law school when 9/11 happened. Signed up for the Academy by the end of the day. Went out and married a firefighter a few years later."

Rueful smile.

"I didn't know her," I said, "but I've heard she was a really good lady."

"She was." Deep breath. Carefully folding up and pushing away memories. Grief is messy.

Nolo stretched and nuzzled her head against the lieutenant's hand. No surprise. I'd already seen she had good emotional radar.

Carla gave the cat a scratch, and she started to purr. "Anyhow, bottom line, I've always gotten along well with lawyers."

"Most of us do try to do the right thing." I took a sip of my coffee. "I'm leaning hard on Al and Vince."

She didn't need to know it didn't seem to be working very well, at least according to Ethan Storey. The earnest was enough, since I had a decent plan—if I could just pull it off in time.

"I don't doubt it," she said.

As she petted the cat, I had a thought. "You know, part of the problem is, they have no idea where Doremus is."

"Nobody does."

"Really?"

"Really. After they got pinched that first day, I looked up everyone else."

"And even *you* can't find him?" I stared at her over my coffee.

"Nope. He's not in any of the databases. I'm sure he changed his name, and he must have also changed his social."

"Which can happen," I said, "but it's not fast and easy."

"Right. There's usually a record."

"Almost always. And if there's not, someone in law enforcement should at least be able to find a few breadcrumbs."

"I've reached out to everyone I know." Irritated twist of her mouth. "No tracks."

"So he could be dead under a rock somewhere, hiding in plain sight—or creeping in the background."

"Any or all of the above." Her eyes sharpened on mine. "You're worried he might have been behind the crash."

"Only a little, but yeah."

"I can't be a hundred percent sure because there's no such thing, but everything I know suggests the local druggies are the best theory."

"Really? Trying to kill a lawyer over losing one poor little girl?"

"Oh, yeah. Some of these guys are nuts. And they're all about money and making statements. This fits pretty well."

Not a false note in her voice.

"That's soothing, I think."

"It was intended to be. As best I can tell, there's no continuing threat. Though, of course, you're keeping a very close eye to your safety."

"I'll have my eyes on the rearview mirror for a long time."

"And friends and family keeping an eye on you too."

"All the time."

"Not a bad thing."

"Nope." I took a breath. Surprised to find myself a little wobbly.

Carla Luciano studied me for a moment. "Look, trauma's a weird thing. You're going to be off-balance at the strangest times. It will pass."

Took me a moment to find my voice. "I sure hope so."

"It will. Just remind yourself it's a normal part of the process. You've been attacked and hurt, and you don't just jump up all right the next day."

"Sounds like you know this one. The glass frag thing?"

"One of 'em." She clearly didn't want to delve too much into her own experience, whether out of respect for mine, or her own desire to avoid messy emotion in the middle of a workday.

I nodded.

Carla shook her head and took the last bite of her cannoli. Looked longingly at the plate.

"Want some to take home?"

"Not if it'll leave you with only that antioxidant bundt."

"Don't worry," I said. "I can spare a few."

"Nice. My daughter likes them too."

"I'd expect nothing less."

Shared smile.

Five minutes later, she left with a plastic container of pastries, after giving me the rundown on proper use of the aloe cream, and Nolo one last ear scratch.

Like so many other things in my life, it could have been a lot worse.

CHAPTER THIRTY-THREE
THE SORCERER'S APPRENTICE

A wonderful dinner of Mexican lasagna (otherwise known as cultural appropriation casserole), a little family time, and a decent night's sleep later, we arrived at Friday morning with wedding weekend coming up fast.

My day began pretty hopefully, with confirmation of an appointment I hoped would settle the Al and Vince matter once and for all. Sure, the only time this could happen was at eleven a.m. on Sunday, just hours before the vows, but it was still a very strong plan.

I would just have to have faith.

Well, have faith, and make sure everything was lined up for the high-wire act.

Drop-off was uneventful and fun, with Corinna, Brian, and I cheerfully chattering about our—and our kids'—respective wedding getups.

On the way back, I noticed a big dark SUV in my rearview mirror again on two different streets. Paranoia, nothing more,

I was sure.

If I was going to freak out every time I saw a big SUV, I wouldn't last long in suburbia.

Anyhow, the wedding gear talk had reminded me I had a mission. When I got home, I put in a rush order for a white tuxedo shirt for Michael to replace the one that didn't make it out of the water. It would arrive Sunday morning, but that was fine.

Otherwise, Michael was wearing his kilt with his white oxford shirt. Which would be close but no cigar.

After placing the order and answering a couple of emails, my head was hurting and my stomach twisting again. I was just getting ready to nap when I got a real surprise visitor: Adam Dix. The junior assistant state's attorney appeared at my door with a scraggly bouquet from the minimart down the road.

"I was supposed to bring you something, right?" he asked, holding out the flowers.

"It's very kind," I said, taking them. "Let me put these in water."

As Dix walked into the house, Nolo hopped up on the little occasional table, knocking off my car keys as she landed.

Scotchie rushed out of the kitchen, demanding attention too. Full court press.

To his credit, Dix didn't flinch. He just laughed and tried to pet one animal with each hand. It didn't work but that wasn't the point.

It told me everything I needed to know about ASA Adam Dix.

"Would you like some coffee? Maybe a baked good?"

"You wouldn't have any tea?"

"Sure. Ginger okay?"

"Yes please. I'm trying to be healthy in the New Year. Better skip the baked goods."

"I have an antioxidant bundt from Alyssa Marchand's recipe. Butternut squash and lots of nutrients."

"Oh, that would be wonderful!"

Someone on whom to pawn off Kryssie's horrid cake? Major win! "I'll send you home with some too."

"Wow. Thank you."

Nolo gave Dix a sniff and a once-over and then strutted off. Scotchie, though, was more than happy to settle in for a good attention session, licking Dix's fingers and thumping his tail on the floor. By the time I'd steeped two cups of ginger-orange tea and set a generous slice of bundt on a plate, with most of the rest of the cake wrapped in foil to go, he was sitting on the couch with Scotchie's head resting on his knee, staring into the soulful brown eyes.

"Guess you made friends," I said.

"Oh, he just smells Marshall, my cat. I have a big tabby tom. Vet thinks he's part Maine coon, but we'll never know for sure."

"Nice," I said, setting the tray down on the table. "The tea's pretty hot, but the bundt is edible. I think."

He took the plate and fork, and cut off a bite, chewing cautiously. "Um, this is—um, good."

"I'm sure it's dreadful, but I didn't make it. A PTA acquaintance and influencer fan did. I'm not sure if she was trying to help or one-up me."

"It's not terrible," he said. "Moist, and there's a little bit of glaze on it. But not very sweet or..."

"Here," I said. I picked up the honey bear and squeezed a bunch on the cake. "Maybe that'll help."

Adam Dix laughed like a misbehaving little kid. "That'll work. Thanks, Ms. Adair."

"Nobody eats bad food in my house," I assured him. "So what's up?"

"I'm still worried about Vince," he said. "He disappeared again at least once this week, and I keep finding him sifting through old records. And he's been searching online databases, which you know he never does."

"He sure doesn't," I agreed. "He's one of the most low-tech humans I know."

"And I know he and Al got taken in. And that you got them out."

I almost dropped my cup. "How?"

"Got a cousin who's a uniform. Told me because he knows how much I revere Vince." Dix took a bite of the honey-covered bundt. "Much better."

"I won't say I told you so."

"You can." He chomped a generous chunk. "This is actually pretty good."

"Good. You can take some with you." I patted the cake container. "You've got honey, right?"

"Bought some when I geared up for the New Year's resolution."

"Then you're all set."

"So you're watching out for Vince and Al?"

"They're my clients, so yeah, as much as I can."

"Do you have any idea what Vince is looking for?"

"Yeah," I said. "And I'd better not tell you."

"No?"

Pretty much the last thing I needed was Adam Dix joining the hunt for Ronald Doremus. Dix was a very nice, very young—emphasis on the young—guy who was miles away from a clue. The fact that he was here happily petting the dog and snarfing influencer bundt told me so. It would never have occurred to him that I wouldn't tell him what he wanted to know, and certainly not that I might have an agenda of my own.

Or that I might be a threat to him.

Not that I was, of course. It would have been like stepping on a bunny rabbit.

But somebody needed to teach this kid some street smarts. I would have thought Vince was taking care of it. Probably too distracted by the whole Ethan Storey situation.

"No," I replied. "It's better you don't know everything going on here. If only so you don't have guilty knowledge."

"There's guilty knowledge to have?"

"Not really, but why take a chance?" I picked up my tea mug.

"Do you have any idea why they decided to come after Storey now?" he asked.

"Probably the twenty-year mark. It came last summer." I shrugged. "Milestones will do that."

"You didn't say anniversary." His face crimped into a puzzled expression.

"No. An anniversary is a happy thing. I never use that word for something like this."

"Oh. I get it. My mom gets weird every year on the day my dad…"

"Bet you do too."

Squirm. Eyes focused on his cup. "Yeah, I do. Drunk driver. Why I'm a prosecutor, actually."

"I'm sorry for your loss. And glad you chose to deal with it like this."

"In my family, we say: don't just sit there and cry—do something about it."

"I think I like your family." I smiled.

He smiled back. "So what do I do about Vince?"

"Probably nothing. Just keep a subtle eye on him, and cover anything he misses if you can."

"Subtle eye?"

"Well, yeah."

"Could somebody be following him?"

"Why?"

"It's weird. I've seen a dark SUV out of the corner of my eye a couple times when we were talking on the portico. I keep telling myself it's nothing."

"There are an awful lot of dark SUVs around here."

"I know. That's why I think I'm imagining things because of everything that's happening." Dix speared the last bite of bundt with his fork and swept it over the plate, soaking up the remaining honey. "Actually, I like this."

He liked the honey, I suspected. They probably don't feed him at home.

"Look," I said. "I don't know everything that's going on here. If you see that SUV again, try to get its tag."

"I could even run it."

"But you're not going after them, okay?"

Adam Dix gave me a mutinous look, clearly unhappy at my stopping his amateur detective fantasy.

"Give me your word. Neither Vince—nor I—need to be worrying about you."

"I guess." He almost pouted. "But if I see it following Vince, I'm tailing it."

"No," I said, "you're calling it the hell in."

"Oh, all right."

A faint note of relief in his tone suggested Dix liked the idea of being a hero far more than the reality of tracking a threat.

Soon after, I sent him on his way with the bundt.

Better him than me.

CHAPTER THIRTY-FOUR
BUT WAIT, THERE'S MORE...

After Dix left, I opened my laptop for a casual, just-in-case look at my email.

A long and painful half-hour later, I'd fielded yet more good wishes, whining and demands disguised as such, and a few impressively intrusive questions.

It was a real relief to see Madge coming up the walk, even if she was carrying yet another baked goods box.

"Hey," I said. "Please don't make me eat."

"Why not?" She gave me a concerned once-over.

"Screen stuff. Yet more email. But at least I got Michael's new shirt ordered."

"Cutting it close."

"They overnight—we've used them before." I motioned her inside.

Even after we were settled with drinks—coffee for her, and me with yet more of the dreaded ginger tea—the little worry furrows in her brow hadn't relaxed.

"Okay," I said. "Wedding jitters or something else?"

"I guess it's wedding jitters to wonder if you're going to get to have a wedding at all…"

"Oh, Madge." I put my tea down and took her hand.

"What?"

"I know you have a plan, but Professor Munroe told me she wants absolute assurances or she's going to call it off."

"And I'm going to have those assurances in hand by go time," I told her. One nice thing about being an excellent lawyer, not to mention assassin, is that I'm very good at sounding absolutely confident and credible.

Of course, Madge knows this better than most, and it didn't work as well with her.

Usually.

Today, whether because she was desperate for any reassurance or because I'm that good—my money is on the former—she simply nodded. "Please God you're right."

"Let's just say I'm bringing in a little help from a higher power."

"Higher how?"

"Someone Al and Vince will definitely listen to. And who will stop them cold. I don't want to say anymore because I'm terrified too."

"But you're reasonably sure?"

"It's the absolute best I can get." I took a careful sip of the tea. Ginger mint. I supposed it wasn't terribly offensive. At this point, the only ginger I wanted to see was the one on *Gilligan's Island*, but it did help the nausea a little.

"Okay." Her face relaxed. "If you're confident, I'm confident."

"Good. We'll be fine. I might need some help with the makeup, though, unless you want to have people wondering who beat up your flower girl."

"I think the Bothwell House has a makeup artist. They're throwing all kinds of extras at us because the event planner is the daughter of one of Al's old colleagues."

"That's really nice."

"Maybe." Madge scowled. "I think they think we're cute. You know, all that second chance romance hoopla."

"They're not wrong. You are pretty wonderful and adorable." A bit of a blush crept up her cheekbones. "I'll tolerate that from you—once. But it's kind of insulting."

"Oh, it is not. Everybody wants to believe love can happen to anyone at any time. And do you really want to live in a world where we don't believe that?"

"I guess not. But why do Al and I have to be the poster kids for late-life romance?"

"Because you'll be standing there holding the bouquet Sunday. There are a lot worse things."

Madge held my gaze for a moment. "And you're going to make sure some of them don't happen."

"You bet I am."

"Okay." She drank some of her coffee. Toyed with the lid of the box. "I've got shortbread if you want one."

"Not now." I nodded to my teacup. "This stuff is at least starting to work. Let's give it a chance."

"You may need it when I tell you what else I've learned."

"Why?"

"How's the investigation of the aquarium killing going?"

"Well, let's just say nobody's in a big hurry to find out who took out Eric Egan, considering."

"Understandably. But he's even worse than you think."

What could possibly—don't ask the universe that question right now!

"Okay," I said, waiting.

"Professor Munroe has learned something truly disturbing."

It had to be bad if it disturbed Professor Munroe.

"Eric Egan was Cathie Holman's sixth attacker."

Well, I doubt anyone had *that* on their bingo card.

I almost did a spit-take with my tea.

"Come on," I sputtered. "How could he be Ronald Doremus?"

"He served his time in juvie and was then taken in by a Jesuit order that works to help troubled young men. They gave him a new name to go with his new life."

"New social security number too?"

"Apparently so. There's a way to do that, but it's not easy."

"It's not, and it's usually traceable—eventually."

"So this is going to come out, then?" Madge wrapped her hands around her mug.

"Oh, I'm pretty sure it will." I tried for another sip of tea. It didn't help. Jesuits, I thought. A religious order with all the relevant connections. The perfect explanation for how Doremus, now Egan, ended up in the priesthood. And for how he went so very bad.

"It's not a coincidence that the last name, Egan, was that of an archbishop, was it?" I asked.

"Probably not."

Likely intended as a tribute, not an ironically appropriate callback, though it turned out that way. And the church had to keep moving Doremus around because his continued bad behavior was their mistake. Not just morally, but quite possibly legally.

The bad story just kept getting worse.

Not just for Doremus's victims, though they were the only ones I cared about, but for the church that had supposedly rehabilitated him.

"The name should have been a clue," I said. That, and the very thin dossier we'd been given. We knew it was a trouble sign that he just seemed to appear out of nowhere at the seminary. We just didn't know what kind of trouble.

"Maybe," Madge said. "But it's not the first time a commission came in with an unclear background."

"True. The sisters weren't doing a background check for a job, they were trying to determine if he met the criteria for removal."

"And you don't need to know what elementary school he attended for that."

"Exactly," I agreed.

"And he did meet the criteria. He was only free because he gave evidence against the pastor, and everyone was convinced he'd lured children to him, at the very least."

Madge took a deep breath. "And probably far worse. We don't have to worry about whether he deserved it, anyhow."

"True. But now we have a whole new field of possible suspects," I said. "Anyone connected to the Holman case needs a look."

"They do if they knew," Madge agreed. "But how would they know?"

"How did Professor Munroe—" I started, then realized what a foolish a question it was. "Without her special access, though?"

"Does he look much like he did as a kid?"

"I really don't think so."

"So now what?" Madge asked.

"Darned if I know," I said.

Her phone buzzed. "Yikes. Al and I are doing a walkthrough at the Bothwell House in an hour and he's driving."

"Go, go—we'll talk later." *Thank heaven for wedding planning,* I thought.

Just as well.

I needed time to think.

I tried to remember the case file Vince had shown me years ago, when he was explaining why he pushed to treat most mid-teenagers as adults. All I remembered of Ronald Doremus's mugshot was a lot of messy dark hair and a bad case of cystic acne. The photo didn't matter much, anyway. It had been taken after a night in the lockup, when the arresting officers had made it known the suspects were in for beating up a young girl.

Eric Egan had short dark hair and a well-trimmed beard... which, now you mention it, would have hidden the acne scars and obscured his facial shape. I tried to think if there were any similarities that would stand out. Doremus had been short and thin, described derisively as a runt, and he got such a good deal because it had seemed like he was just tagging along with stronger and more dangerous people.

Eric Egan had been short and chunky, and he carried himself with a trying-too-hard overconfidence that could have been cover for insecurity or fear. Not without cause, even with what we'd originally known about him.

I'd never known Ronald Doremus, and really, I had no realistic way to connect the two. What I could not say with any certainty was whether someone who'd known him would have recognized the boy in Eric Egan.

Or what might happen if they had.

Actually, it was entirely possible we knew what had happened.

Cathie Holman was at least as good a motive for murder as the New Jersey case. Maybe better.

The real shocker for me was, this was my third connection to the aftermath of the Holman case. Not just Al and Vince…but something a good bit closer to home.

One of my first commissions in New Haven had been Cade MacAvoy, the boy at the center of the Holman case. I'd made the poison and was almost ready to deliver it when Madge called to tell me the client didn't want to go ahead. She was as stunned as I was. As far as either of us knew, no one had ever called off a contract. Once you commit and send payment, jeopardy, as we lawyers like to say, has attached. You're in.

No refunds, obviously, but apparently in extremely rare cases, the commission can just simply be cancelled. With the assumption that no one will ever discuss the matter again.

Unless they'd like it to be reactivated…or worse.

No explanation or other word on the Cade MacAvoy commission ever came down from the Mothers. A few weeks later, the chief mean girl, Char Torrey, shot Cade and burned his house down while they were both still inside and alive. Being a prosecutor, I had access to the reports, and all anyone need know is they got their hell on the way out.

If I wondered who'd wanted Cade dead, and why they changed their mind, it no longer mattered, and I knew enough not to ask too many questions, anyway.

And now, Ronald Doremus had quite literally dropped into the middle of my life.

There's more going on here. Has to be.

It's a small world, but not that small.

Scotchie nudged me out of my ruminations. He had that "out or else" look.

And trust me, nobody wants to clean up Scotchie's "or else."

On the way back in, I walked right into another one of those evil rays of sunshine. I stumbled back to the living room and hid under my heated blanket with Nolo again.

Someday I was going to feel better.

This time, though, the shivering wasn't all from the concussion.

I dragged myself through pickup, and since it was Friday, parked Daniel in front of the PBS Kids videos and returned to my blanket. Daniel curled up beside me, and Nolo perched on the back of the couch.

That's how Michael found us when he came home with a big bag of Chinese takeout and a bigger smile. Couldn't think of a better way to end this brutal week.

CHAPTER THIRTY-FIVE
WEDDING EVE BLUES

Saturday morning turned out to be the one thing we hadn't had in the last two weeks: normal.

Michael and I slept late with Daniel cuddled between us, Nolo on my pillow, and Scotchie at our feet. It was crowded and messy and absolutely wonderful.

So was Michael's cooking pancakes, making a disaster area of the kitchen in the service of a delicious brunch. Since it was a cloudy morning, I didn't get the light-sensitivity nausea, and I was able to really enjoy it.

Michael and Daniel headed out for their usual weekend visit to the hardware store, and I decided to really get myself back in order, with a good hard walk on the treadmill, and some major hair and beauty time.

Once again, the walk really helped. Yay for endorphins.

"I'm back, bitches!" I yelled in the empty exercise room.

Only a little sheepish.

Felt too good to be myself again to be embarrassed.

Suddenly, the "I'm back" sparked something else in the corner of my bruised brain.

Did anyone else know Ronald Doremus was back?

Madge and I had only just found out who Eric Egan really was, after all. I'd been going on the assumption he was targeted because of his most recent past life and his current work that put him in contact with children. But what if someone else knew who he was, and wanted him dead for his earliest offense?

It was certainly possible.

No, it wasn't visually obvious that Doremus had become Egan. The boy had been reedy and looked young for his age, where the chunky Egan seemed older. But, unlike Al and Vince's target, Ethan Storey, Doremus hadn't looked frightened in his booking photo. He'd seemed bored, with a little sneer at the top of his hairless upper lip. Egan had worn a little mustache and a scruff, and the sneer would not have been so easily noticeable.

Besides, would we have ever seen him with a bored and contemptuous expression?

Violet the Smart Speaker switched to the hot Taylor Swift song from last summer, and I realized I had seen Egan looking just that way, once. During the curriculum meeting at the beginning of the school year. Like it was a major hardship for him to explain the proposal and the benchmarks to us. Corinna and I had both asked questions about what we could do to foster our children's reading habits—Daniel and Cherise arrived at school with basic reading skills, as many kids in language-rich homes do—and Egan had talked down to us.

With a sneer I now recognized as an echo of Doremus's.

Someone in that meeting might have recognized it too. Sure, New Haven County is a huge population center, but it's a relatively small area, and a relatively small world. And the booking photos of Doremus and the others had been all over the media at the time it happened. It was possible.

I didn't know anyone with any connections to the Holman case, or at least I didn't think I did. But would I know? It wasn't the sort of thing people talked about.

My best friends were out, thankfully. Corinna was from a

Harlem church family, Brian grew up in Yonkers, and Pete was from Great Barrington, Massachusetts. But a lot of the people in Alcott were longtime locals, generational clans.

Which meant there were an awful lot of potential contenders.

Despite the wonderful rush of the workout, and the adorable sight of Nolo happily watching me from the windowsill, my good mood drained away at the exhausting thought of tracking down everyone who might have a connection.

This was actually a lot worse than the possibility that Doremus might have been alive and around. One person—even one really evil person—was a lot easier to worry about than an entire circle of family and friends. All it would have taken is one relative or friend of the Holman family to recognize Eric Egan as Doremus and set the plot in motion.

For starters, the person in question could have called the commission on Egan. I'd been going on the general assumption that the client was from the New Jersey parish. But now, I had to accept it could just as easily be somebody local.

Maybe even somebody who was on our aquarium trip.

The good news was, there was every possibility a person with a strong motive who was not Brian or Pete was on the train. The bad news was the pool (no pun intended) was close to a dozen people.

And some of them had to have dark SUVs.

With Doremus out of the picture, and the possibility somebody had called the commission on him because of Cathie Holman rather than his later life, I had to wonder.

Probably a good thing I had to spend the rest of the day getting everybody ready for the wedding. It was better to be anxious about whether Michael's new dress shirt would arrive in time than to vex about some of the other things going on out there.

Or what might be just beyond my line of vision.

CHAPTER THIRTY-SIX
ON THE WEDDING EVE

While Al and Madge had decided against the traditional bachelor or jack-and-jill parties and rehearsal dinner, they did want a happy family night before the wedding at their favorite Italian restaurant.

Very New Haven County.

Everybody has a favorite red-sauce spot, and theirs is Molina's in Unity, the next town over, because it's where they went on their first date. We suspect it's because they didn't want the whole cast playing cupid, which we would not have done—honest.

Well, there's always a possibility one or two of us might have had a craving for Molina's famous gnocchi alla vodka...and just casually dropped in a good word, so they were probably right.

That night, though, the alla vodka was out in the open, and everyone settled in for a good evening, even if it was going to be an early night for those of us with young kids. And for those of us who were still fighting concussion fatigue.

Madge and Al didn't have a real seating chart, but they mixed up couples so we could all converse with different people. I ended up between Madge's son and Brian, which turned out to be plenty of fun, since they share my guilty glee in trashy procedurals.

We spent most of the evening in a deep dive on the latest season of 9-1-1, parsing the details of a particularly shocking character death, the sort of conversation I could never have with Corinna, or even Michael, whose tastes are just a little too elevated.

Before dessert, Brian and I ended up alone while the immediate family posed for pics.

"How are you holding up?" he asked, nodding to my Sicilian lemon soda. "Still concussed?"

"Doc says it takes a while." I motioned to the softly lit room. "Light sensitivity is still a problem, but not in rooms like this."

"So you'll be fine tomorrow night."

"Yeah." I took a sip of my soda. "No drinkie for a while, though."

"Well, that sucks."

"Yeah. I don't think I've ever been at a wedding without at least having a glass of champagne." I shrugged. "But if that—and these bruises—are the worst…"

"Yep. They haven't caught the guy?"

"No. Cops think probably the dealer of a client I got into drug court."

"Ugh. Scary."

"Definitely. We've had a bad couple of weeks."

His face tightened. "No kidding. Are they any closer to an arrest in the aquarium thing?"

I heard something in his voice, and I watched him carefully as I spoke. "Not as far as I know."

"Ah."

"Pretty tough on you guys and Zooey, being up there when it happened," I said, watching for his reaction.

"Yeah, it was." His wince suggested a lot of things, few of them good. I didn't think there was any way he or Pete could know Egan was Doremus...but Egan was more than bad enough to get his ticket punched.

"Do you—"

"Hey, you two, whatever it is, it can wait!" Corinna appeared behind us, cappuccino in hand. "They're bringing out the dessert tray!"

"All things stop for cannoli," I said.

"Bring it on," Brian agreed.

Whatever was going on with Brian and Pete would have to wait until after the cannoli, and the wedding. And I assumed it could.

Sometimes I amaze myself with my miscalculations.

CHAPTER THIRTY-SEVEN
CAN'T KILL YOUR WAY OUT

Wedding (and Big Game) Day dawned sunny, and once again, dangerously cold.

Not a problem for the wedding party, since we were going from the house to the car and the car to the Bothwell House. A minor issue for me on my first errand of the day, though.

I told Michael there were some last-minute wedding things to do, which was strictly true because if I didn't make this short trip with Al and Vince, there would be no wedding. At this point, hours away, I wasn't even admitting the possibility of failure.

And I wasn't accepting delivery on the twinge of fear in my stomach when I noticed a dark SUV a few cars back in my rearview. It was me. And the concussion.

Ronald Doremus was dead.

Anyone who'd known and wanted him would have no motive to come after me.

Would they?

Anyhow, the question of the aquarium murder and my crash

would still be there tomorrow. Today was all about clearing the path for the wedding—and then enjoying the day.

At least I hoped it would be.

Promptly at ten thirty a.m., I pulled up at Vince's New Haven apartment building, to scoop him and Al up for our little trip to the shore. Old Weymouth is a small waterfront community tucked between New Haven and the next major town. It's an elegant enclave hidden in plain sight, with old Victorian mansions along a boulevard facing Long Island Sound.

The boulevard was probably wide and gracious when it was built more than a hundred years ago. For modern cars and drivers, it's close and crowded, but the mansions are still relatively far apart, with long drives winding around back, the better to clear the view from the big front windows.

Each house had a sign and a name, like the much fancier ones on Martha's Vineyard. A few had company names, the priceless old buildings repurposed for commerce. The place I was looking for had been repurposed too, but the signage wasn't nearly as fancy.

I would have missed it, if I hadn't been driving slowly and squinting hard.

Vince and Al squirmed like misbehaving six-year-olds when they saw the simple wooden sign, with the cross and angel.

"Convent of the Contemplative Sisters?" Vince asked.

"What the—" Al started.

"Ride with me, fellas. I'm hoping we can settle this once and for all."

I parked in a gravel lot and pulled my puffer tighter around me as I herded the guys up the flagstone path to a heavy wooden door, then rang the big brass bell.

Inside, in a serviceable tiled room that was probably once the scullery, an older lady in a black dress with a striped apron and a short shoulder-length veil welcomed us with a careful, and only slightly suspicious, gaze. "You're new."

"Yes, ma'am," Al said. Vince muttered a "Yes, S'ter" that probably came from his Catholic school boyhood.

"I called a few days ago," I said. "Arranged to speak with Mother Michael?"

"Oh, yes." The caution dissolved into a gentle smile. "She agrees it's very important and she's willing to give you a few minutes. Go to the screen there and wait. I'll tell her you're here."

We turned to what appeared to be a small visiting area, with a bench and a couple of chairs in front of a window, screened like a confessional, only larger.

As we sat, Vince whispered, "Who…" and Al gave me a puzzled stare.

"Give it a minute," I said.

It was maybe thirty seconds before a panel behind the screen slid back, revealing the image of what could have been a medieval nun behind the wooden lace.

"Hello, Detective Kaufman and State's Attorney Scupper. It's good to see you under better circumstances."

The voice carried the lilt of a young girl, but there was a serene depth to her tone. What I could see of her eyes, round and bright blue, reflected the same calm.

Al and Vince startled at her first word, then stared.

"Cathie?" Al asked.

"It's Mother Michael now. When I joined the sisters, I took the name of the most powerful Archangel—God's Warrior—because I needed the strength. Only after many years of prayer did I realize it takes far more strength to forgive."

"Forgive." Vince shot me a glare.

"Yes, Mr. Scupper." A breath, and when she continued, her voice held a trace of a smile. "Mrs. Adair asked me to speak with you two. To ask you to stop."

"Stop?" Al asked.

"Leave Ethan to God. I'm asking you directly to honor your respect for me and what happened to me, and stop pursuing him."

"But, Sister—" Vince remonstrated.

"Vengeance is mine, saith the Lord. Not either of you two."

"That's not the point," Al said. "There's a debt…"

"And it will be paid. But not to us."

"You can forgive?" Vince asked.

"I can and I have."

"Really?" Al asked.

"I was a mess of bitterness and hatred and misery when I arrived here almost twenty years ago. I almost did something very foolish because of those feelings."

Her gaze rested on me for just a moment too long. Was *she* the one who'd called—and cancelled—the commission on Cade MacAvoy? And how much did she know?

"But in all this praying time," the nun continued, "I've come to realize the only way forward is to forgive. To put love into the world instead of hate."

"Oh." Vince slumped a bit.

Al followed suit.

"If I can forgive them—and him—how can you two do anything less?"

They both gave reluctant nods.

"Give me your word. It ends here."

"All right," Al growled.

"Yes, Sister." Vince had probably had exactly the same tone and posture as a misbehaving student sixty years ago.

"Thank you." She turned to me. "And thank you, Mrs. Adair, for bringing them here. Hopefully, we can all go forward in love and peace."

"Well," I said, "Al's about to do just that tonight."

"Oh?"

"He and a dear friend of mine are getting married."

Even through the screen, her radiant smile warmed the room. "How wonderful! You don't mind my wishing you blessings and offering a prayer for health and happiness, do you?"

"Not a bit, Mother." Al returned the smile. "Jews appreciate good wishes too."

"Good." She rose. "And of course, I'll continue to offer prayers for you too, Mr. Scupper. And you, Mrs. Adair. You've truly been an instrument of God today."

Unintentional irony? Or deliberate acknowledgment of me as an instrument of justice?

"Well," I said, feeling shy and embarrassed, "now I need to go be a flower girl."

Mother Michael wished us well again and walked away, and the older sister showed us out.

Outside, crossing the gravel parking lot, the guys tried to glare at me. And failed miserably.

"Nice moment, Grace," Al said finally.

"Thanks," Vince added.

"You gave her your word. And I want it too."

"Of course," Al said.

"I promised a nun, for God's sake," Vince said. "That's more than enough."

"Good. Now, let's go get this guy married."

CHAPTER THIRTY-EIGHT
IT ENDS HERE

O n the way back, we stopped at the florist and picked up the boutonnieres—dusty pink roses to match Madge's bouquet—and headed to Vince's. His building has under-ground parking, so I turned down into the garage. There was a dark SUV in the line behind us again, but it was Sunday brunch time in New Haven. Could have been anything.

I pulled up to the elevator bank. Make it easy for them.

"You guys going to be okay till go time?" I asked as they climbed out.

"Sure." Al grinned. "James Bond marathon on DudeTV."

"No Big Game pregame?"

Vince snorted. "You may recall the Patriots lost two weeks ago."

"I don't," I said, throwing on my hazards and popping the trunk so they could get the flower box. I got out to help with doors. "I'm married to a Jets fan."

"That's right," Al said. "My condolences."

"He makes up for it in other areas."

We were sharing a chuckle when I caught movement just at the edge of my vision and turned to see JakesPop standing at the entry door.

With a gun.

"What's so damn funny?" he snapped. "How can you laugh, knowing Ethan Storey is still out there? That he's going to be out there…"

"Just talking football, Larry," Al said. "Come on."

"We've done all we can," Vince added. "And so have you."

"Larry?" I asked, pointlessly, as my mind went back to the police reports. Larry Holman—father of Cathie. And grandfather of Jake, apparently through his other daughter. The lucky one.

Oh, holy hell.

JakesPop.

He'd been here all along.

Apparently not nearly as useless as we'd thought.

How much did he know—or how much did he think he knew—about Al and Vince?

And me?

First, I reminded myself, worry about the gun. I can get my questions answered later.

"You're just going to go get married and live happily ever after, aren't you?" Larry asked Al. "Like it never happened."

"Mr. Holman," I cut in, as weird as it sounded to call him by a real name, "we've just been to see Mother Michael, and—"

"That's not her name! My girl is Cathie."

"She's Mother Michael now," I continued in my court-room-command tone, hoping to calm him. "And she convinced Al and Vince that she doesn't want vengeance."

"But maybe I do."

"And coming after *us* is going to accomplish that?" Al asked, putting up his hands in the universal *calm down* gesture.

"We're on your side." Vince held out his hands too and took a half step.

"Don't move."

"Don't do this," I said.

"You?" Larry Holman wheeled on me, aiming the weapon right at my midsection. "What do you know about any of this?"

Okay, that was a good question.

Means he didn't know just how much I did know...and what I'd been hired to do.

That would help. If we got out of this confrontation.

"I know Vince and Al don't deserve this. And that your daughter wants to stay with God...and leave her remaining attacker to Him."

"You should have let them take care of Storey," Larry said. "I'd finally gotten rid of the other one, so—"

"The other one." I watched his face as I put it together. He pushed Egan off the train. At least Brian and Pete were innocent—and safe. I said the names: "Ronald Doremus, who'd become Eric Egan."

"Damn right. I knew when I saw that smirk of his at the curriculum meeting. I'll never forget that snarky, suck-up face."

"And you wanted to make sure you never saw it again," I said.

"I paid good money to have him taken out—and they didn't move fast enough."

They who?

And then it hit me.

They—me.

My jaw dropped.

Not only had he killed Egan—he was the client who'd taken the commission on him.

There was no way he could know I was the sister assigned to the case, could he?

"What do you mean?" I asked, hanging on to command presence. I still had a shot at brazening our way out of this.

"Never mind. It didn't happen." He brushed it off with a quick hand gesture. "You saw me. I couldn't leave a witness."

"I didn't see a damn thing!" I snapped back. "How did you think—"

"What you said when we were at the gym with the kids the next day. I thought you were threatening me."

"If I threaten you, you'll know it," I hissed.

"I had to get rid of you," JakesPop said.

Get rid of me. I flicked a glance at the large black SUV behind him. A noticeable dent on the bumper…and I bet they'd find red Infiniti paint in it.

Suddenly all I could see was red. I stepped toward him. "You son of a bitch! You almost left my son without a mother!"

"Grace, honey," Al cut in, touching my arm. "He's still got a gun."

I took a breath. Processed.

As I did, Larry Holman stared at me. I realized my move had brought me under one of the sickly fluorescent lights, which had to emphasize my bruises. Had to remind him of another battered female face.

The gun wavered.

The moment gave me just enough time to come up with a plan that might just give us all a chance to finish this cleanly and safely.

"He may have a gun," I said, "but I've got Don Nunzio."

The color drained from Larry's face and his hand holding the gun dropped. "What?"

"I am defending Mr. Imperiale's niece. And the Don thinks the crash was an attack on him."

"If anything happens to her," Vince nodded to me. "or if she tells him she knows who came after her…"

"I wouldn't want to be you," Al finished.

For a few very long breaths, we all stared at each other.

Standoff.

Then Larry asked: "So what happens now?"

"You put that thing down and go on with your life, and I forget what I just heard," I said.

"And so do we," Vince agreed.

"You're getting a freebie on Egan," Al reminded him.

"And me." I gave him the look of death.

"It's not—" Larry started.

"It's going to have to be enough." My tone was cold and harsh. "It's time for the vengeance to stop. Mother Michael doesn't want it. And Ethan Storey has spent the last fifteen years serving meals to the homeless, volunteering with a group that keeps ex-cons out of trouble, and feeding feral cats. He's trying to pay his debt. Let God decide when he's done."

Larry lowered the gun. "And that's it?"

"Unless you give us a reason for it not to be," I said. "I'm not too into vengeance."

"After talking to your daughter, I'm not either." Vince studied Larry with a laser-sharp gaze, and flicked a glance to Al.

"You haven't seen her, have you?" Al asked.

"Not since she joined the convent. At first she didn't want to see me, and then..."

"You were afraid of what you'd see." Vince nodded. "We fathers don't always know how to back up our girls."

Al nodded. "You could probably get to the convent before visiting hours are over."

"Yeah?"

"Yeah." Al took the gun from him. "Without this."

"Absolutely." Larry took a breath, looked from Al to Vince to me. "Thank you."

"Don't make us regret it." I held his gaze.

"Don't worry." Larry rummaged out his keys. "Is it okay if I—"

"Get outta here," Vince said, taking the gun from Al. "We'll save this for a gun buyback."

Larry started to turn for the car, then looked back to me. "What about Don Nunzio?"

"What about him? There are no surveillance cams on that road, and it's almost impossible to catch a hit-and-run driver if they're not brought in immediately."

A slow nod from Larry.

We watched him put the SUV in gear and drive off.

It was only after he turned for the out ramp that I started shaking.

Al and Vince pulled me in for a hug, and I caught my breath.

"Okay, guys," I said, slowly detaching after a moment, "you've got James Bond, and I've got a bride to pretty up."

They beamed. "See you tonight."

"Time for the happy ending."

CHAPTER THIRTY-NINE
BLESS THE BRIDE—AND THE FLOWER GIRL

Back in my car, I sent a quick text to Madge: "All good. See you soon."

Then, as I put the car in gear, I punched a now-familiar number on my contact list.

"Mrs. Adair?"

Ethan Storey's voice betrayed a certain amount of trepidation.

"I'm calling with good news."

"Oh?"

"I've had a very productive conversation with my clients, and I can say with considerable authority that you won't have to worry about them again. They have given me their word, with the gravity of a sacred vow, that they will no longer pursue vengeance."

"They won't?"

"They won't. Worry about something else."

"That's really good to hear. Thank you."

"It's the right decision for everyone. Let the past bury its dead."

"I hope everyone can find some peace now." He took a long breath. "Even Ronald."

"He was not a good person," I said. It came out before I could stop it.

"Was? Has he changed?" A strong note of disbelief in his tone.

In it to win it now.

"I'm sorry. I guess you didn't know. He's dead."

"Good." Ethan spat the bitter syllable. "When?"

"I'm not entirely certain," I said. It was true. Doremus might have died when his head hit the tank floor…or six minutes later when his brain went dark from lack of oxygen. And the less dangerous information Ethan had while trying to rebuild his life, the better.

"I'd like to say I'm sorry, but…"

"You don't have to lie to me. He was a terrible person before that night, and he became an even worse one after. The world is a much better place without him in it."

"I don't disagree."

"And a better one with you in it," I continued.

"Thank you so much, Mrs. Adair. I'm really glad I got to know you, despite the circumstances."

"So am I." A really decent man. "And by the way, Ethan, I hope you'll come by some night for dinner and meet my husband, son, and Nolo the Cat."

"Yeah?"

"Yeah. You helped save Nolo, so you should get to know her. Maybe a week or so?"

"I'd love to."

"Good. Check your calendar and let me know."

"Will do."

"Now, if you'll excuse me, I have some flowers to throw."

"Good luck and God bless."

By the time I got home, Michael had taken Scotchie for a good walk and set up his food and water bowls to keep him fed and happy until Dom Benedetti's teenage daughter could check on him. Bella was thinking about vet school and loved Scotchie, not to mention the fact that we were paying her twice the going rate for pet-sitting. All good for a night out.

Nolo was coming with us because we couldn't bear to leave her—and the Bothwell House was small-pet friendly.

Michael and I got ourselves dressed, and Daniel into the green velvet shorts suit his great-aunt had bought him for Christmas. Of course, being a very boyish boy, he wasn't thrilled, but we were taking full advantage of what was probably our last chance to dress him up. By next year, he'd be old enough to really push back, and Michael would probably support him.

Then again, he might just want a kilt like his daddy's.

The big redhead was looking damn near irresistible in full dress, the deep-green velvet Prince Charlie coat setting off his hair and green-gold eyes, still fitting just as well as it did on our wedding day. The waistcoat was even a bit loose, thanks to his treadmill habit. And the new shirt had arrived while I was off dealing with Al and Vince. After a quick steam, you'd never know it wasn't fresh from the cleaner's.

As for me, the less said the better. My rose-pink tulle gown was long enough to hide the stitches on my calf, and high enough to cover most of my other bruises, which were fading to ugly gray and green. My headache had receded enough that it didn't hurt to put up my hair in a loose knot. The problem was my face.

Carla Luciano's aloe cream had taken most of the red out of the glass scratches, but that was only half the battle. The black eyes and bruised cheek that had triggered Larry Holman, aka JakesPop, enough to lose his advantage, weren't going anywhere. They were too deep and dark for conventional means. And the beauty arsenal hadn't helped. Several layers of concealer and powder had only made my skin look fake and dirty.

Not cool.

I washed everything off and decided to beg or bribe Madge's makeup artist for help. The Bothwell House had thrown her hair and makeup into the package because they were so glad to have a wedding on Big Game Sunday, and I hoped the artist could find time to patch me up…for a price. A price I was more than willing to pay.

Nolo didn't appreciate being scooped up and popped into the new carrier, and howled a bit on the drive, but she let Daniel soothe her with pets through the mesh and eventually quieted.

At the inn, Michael handed over the car to the valet, and our suitcase to the bellhop—it's nice to be pampered once in a while—while I took Nolo's carrier. Cat in hand, we checked in and looked around.

"The gentlemen, of all ages, are relaxing in the library, sir," the desk attendant told Michael, nodding toward a hallway, then turning to me. "The bride asked that Mrs. Adair go directly to her dressing room as soon as she gets the kitty settled."

"I can do that."

Michael shot me a grin, and moved toward the hallway, Daniel bouncing ahead of him. My heart warmed, as it always did, to see the joy in his face as he watched his son.

I took five minutes to settle Nolo—who was surprisingly calm—in the room. I set out her bowls and box and scooped her up for a quick cuddle before heading downstairs to the party.

As I stepped out of the elevator, I heard my name and saw a tall silver-haired woman in a deep-green velvet suit. The suit, clearly inspired by the original YSL lady tux, was perfectly cut, with the rich, smooth radiance you only see with real silk velvet.

Her grin was just as real—though the green stones at her ears and neck were probably top-notch fakes, because even she couldn't afford diamonds of that size and color.

"Professor Munroe."

"Grace." Her smile faded, but her light-green eyes still gleamed, as she took a very careful look at me. "You did take a bit of a beating."

"I'm hoping Madge's makeup artist can do some magic."

She studied me. "They're very good. I suspect you'll turn out fine."

"I hope."

I waited.

She waited.

At this point, I honestly wasn't sure what she knew. Or what to say.

Finally, she let out a small sigh and spoke. "Do I want to know what you did?"

"Do I want to know how you know I did something?"

"No, you do not."

"All right." I took a breath, looked around the hall, and pulled her into a nearby ladies' room and locked the door.

"Resourceful, if less than elevated." she said with a smile. "Keep it quick. I suspect other people will wish to put this place to its intended use."

"Of course." I nodded. "Here's the deal. You're entitled to know what I did. I brought Al and Vince to see Mother Michael—the former Cathie Holman."

"I know who she is."

I registered that interesting fact but kept my focus on the moment. "She spoke with them and emphasized that she no longer wants or needs vengeance. And she made them make a sacred vow to stop pursuing it."

"Excellent." The warming sunrise smile that had given me such joy as a novice. "Well done."

"I also made them give me their word."

"Even better." Her gaze returned to sharp assessment. "And?"

She knew me too well.

Of course she could tell there was more.

"After that was settled, I had a bit of a run-in with the victim's vengeful father. He, too, will no longer be seeking revenge."

"No?"

"No. He's also given his word and understands all too well the danger of further action."

"How so?"

"Well, he's the one who removed Eric Egan, and I would have very little trouble marshaling enough evidence to prove it."

"I thought the police were writing that off as an unfortunate mishap."

"They appear to be ready to do so. Considering Mr. Egan's history, nobody wants to look too hard at this."

"As it should be."

"I agree. But the idea that he could find himself in jail over one of his daughter's attackers should provide some motivation." Not to mention contending with Don Nunzio, who I didn't want to invoke with the professor. I knew her thoughts on gangsters.

"That will also do nicely. Good work on all counts, as usual."

"Thank you, Professor."

Those lovely clear-green eyes held mine for a moment. "The vengeful father is the one who ran you off the road, isn't he?"

"Yes."

"And you're choosing to let that go, as well?"

"Yes. It was all of a piece."

"I suppose." Her mouth twisted a bit. "I'm not so sure. He did, after all, deliberately harm one of our sisters..."

"Out of fear that I'd expose a killing that will now permanently go unsolved."

"True. But the fact remains he hurt you and walked away."

"I considered that," I admitted. "But anything that happens to him harms his daughter, who has surely suffered more than enough."

"I suppose." The professor studied me with a reflective expression. "Mercy is good. Weakness is not. I will contemplate on this later."

"Later..."

"Don't worry, Grace. Whatever action is to be taken will not be done by you." She put a hand on my arm.

"Thank you."

"Of course." I could almost hear her shift gears as she gave an impish grin and nodded to the door. "Come along, now."

I unlocked the door. "Right. Almost go time."

"I'm very glad the wedding can go forward. Margaret deserves a good man to love her."

"I agree."

"And good friends too, Grace."

"Or at least a nice flower girl," I said, opening the door.

"Indeed." A chuckle as she put a hand on mine. "You probably have a right to know. Mother Michael has a special relationship with us. She is the only client in my experience to call off an assignment."

So I *had* picked up something. "My first assignment in New Haven."

The cancelled contract on Char Torrey's boyfriend, Cade MacAvoy, who died weeks later as her victim in a murder-suicide.

"Yes. And when you asked her to intervene so that Al could marry Margaret with a clear conscience, she was more than happy to help."

"And to send word to you?"

"The Mothers have their ways."

"Thank you."

"How are you, Grace?"

It's a question the Mothers usually don't ask, and never in that tone. She knew there was cause for concern.

"Healing well, as you noted," I said carefully.

"A bit shaken." She wasn't fooled. "This was a hard one."

"It was."

"Give yourself some time, Grace. You had a scare, even if it wasn't related to your calling. But you came through."

"I did." I took a breath, and let it out, trying to steady myself. "If necessary, I can take action on the attack."

"But…" she prompted.

"I'm relieved you don't want me to." I took another breath. "Too relieved."

"And you're afraid of losing your nerve after all this." She held my gaze, her expression sympathetic, her hand warm on my arm.

"Yes."

"Don't worry." The gaze intensified. "We've all had scrapes here and there and come through fine. The Archangel will take care of you. Trust and have faith. You'll be fine."

It's Professor Munroe's little alchemy trick. For the first time since the water landing, I felt truly warm. Confident and on balance too. Probably just the affirmation from the woman I respect so much—but whatever it was, I'd take it.

"Thank you," I said. "I feel better already."

"Thought you might."

She smiled and popped the door open. "Now, let's get in there. We have a wedding to celebrate."

In the bride's room, Madge was at the mirror, with Al's daughter supervising as the makeup artist put the finishing touches on her face. The photographer was taking one of those standard pregame pics, capturing her sitting in front of the big vanity mirror. Madge was a vision, in her 1919 cream silk gown, hair spun into a French twist, an heirloom bracelet pinned in place as a small tiara, perfectly matching in style.

The photographer, a youngish woman, grinned. "I'm going to get one more pic and leave you ladies to it for now. I need to get a few shots of the groomsmen."

"Make sure you get a couple extra of the guy in the kilt," Madge said. "He's hers."

"*Outlander*, much?" the photographer said with a grin.

Madge patted the makeup artist's arm. "Stop fussing over me and fix her up."

The artist, a twentyish girl with a fun blue streak in her hair, gave me a quick, careful look-over. "This is easy. Sit down and let me do my magic."

"Magic is exactly what I need."

"You're in just the right place." She gave me a reassuring smile and started pulling products out of her tackle box.

"We'll leave you to it," said Professor Munroe, herding the photographer to the door.

"Get a couple shots of the guy in the white dinner jacket too," I said, nodding to Professor Munroe. "He's hers."

"He's in a Cary Grant mood tonight," the professor added.

I'd expect nothing less of any man she considers worthy.

CHAPTER FORTY
WITH THIS RUGELACH

After the makeup artist finished with me, Madge and I were alone for moment.

"Looking gorgeous," she assured me.

"Back at you. Not cute," I emphasized, "gorgeous."

"Thank you, Grace. For everything."

"Glad to. And so glad to be here."

As I helped Madge smooth out her veil—no face covering for a second-time bride, just a beautiful cloud of glittery tulle—and handed her the bouquet of dusty-pink roses, I could hear everyone lining up in the hall.

A knock at the door. "Ma, you ready?"

Her son. He and Al's daughter were walking them both up to the judge.

"Am I ever!" she called.

"I'll leave you to your family," I said.

"Thank you, Grace."

"Thank *you*."

I picked up my basket of rose petals and opened the door.

"Give it up for the flower girl!" Al's daughter called as I stepped past her.

That was when I realized I was the only member of the wedding party who hadn't been enjoying some pregame adult beverages.

Judge Harriman, Al and his pals, and the rest of the folks in the hall greeted me with a cheer.

And not a single wince at my bruises. Nice to be normal again.

"Back at ya!" I replied, dropping a curtsy.

More applause.

"Is this a wedding party or the Village People?" Vince asked as he got in line. Between Michael's kilt, the assistant police commissioner's dress blues, the reserve general's full military dress, the judge's robe, and Al's prayer shawl and yarmulke embroidered by Madge, it was a reasonable question.

The ceremony was every bit as moving and joyful as we could have hoped, all of us surrounding Madge and Al as they made their vows.

The candle glow was nothing compared to the light in their eyes.

And this light didn't hurt my head.

At the end, Al stomped on the glass and we all yelled "Mazel tov!"

Joyful pandemonium, hugs and handshakes and back-slaps, and our happy couple running down the aisle.

They were observing the old Jewish tradition of taking an hour alone after the ceremony. None of our business what they might have been up to, and honestly, the cocktail hour was such a great party nobody had the time for salacious speculation.

Three hors d'oeuvre stations, open bar, and plenty of interesting people for good conversation, not to mention a wonderful, joyous energy in the room. It was the best kind of whirlwind.

Corinna and I, and Al's daughter, discovered that we're all fans of the same summer arts festival at Long Wharf and started making plans for a group outing. All the talking made me thirsty, and I headed for the bar for seltzer, or hopefully a decent mocktail. The bartender made me a Shirley Temple. Perfect for the flower girl.

"Tell me all about Carla Luciano."

I turned in response to the voice and tap on the shoulder to find Moira, looking happy and spiffy in a gorgeous, gold-embroidered red satin jacket over a long black dress, with an expression that suggested a crushing tween. Well, Carla was pretty amazing, sending out major Sophia Loren vibes in a wine-colored jersey wrap dress with her salt-and-pepper hair flowing.

"Um, one of Al's trainees. Police Lieutenant, stand-up lady."

"Single?"

"Um, yeah. Widowed—her wife was the first female New Haven firefighter to die in the line. That warehouse collapse five years ago. Left her with a daughter—a tween now. You thinking about a fixup?"

"Yeah," Moira said, taking a sip of what was probably either a gin or vodka tonic, "with me."

"Oh…" I started and quickly stopped myself. Moira and her husband had divorced, amiably, at least five years ago when her younger son started college, and my sense had been she was too busy with her mother's care to think about dating. Maybe she'd been rethinking the whole thing. None of my business, honestly.

Time to be a good, supportive, non-judgmental friend. "That could be great. She's really terrific—and so are you. Why not just enjoy the evening and see what happens?"

"Exactly my thinking, Grace." Moira smiled. "No better place to start something than tonight, when we're already celebrating love and second chances."

"I like it."

Moira took a good slurp of her drink and headed back to the pasta bar, where Carla Luciano was perusing the options with a large glass of red in hand. She turned to me and raised her glass—and I raised mine.

Nice.

"Got a minute, Grace?"

I turned to see Pete and Brian. No food or drinks, and anxious expressions.

Uh-oh.

"Sure. What's up?" I asked, falling in step with them as we passed the cookie table.

"Well," Pete said, glancing at Brian.

"What would we have to do to get confidentiality?" he asked.

I pointed to the table, where rugelach and Scottish shortbread were laid out as a little tease for the big dessert buffet later. "Get a few rugelach."

"Um, okay." Brian scooped up three and put them on a plate.

"Good, now come over here with me." I motioned to a space near the bandstand, which was empty, since most folks were enjoying the various food stations.

We ducked behind one of the big speakers.

I nodded to Brian's plate. "Okay, give me a cookie."

He handed it over, and I accepted it, and took a nibble.

"Apricot-almond. Nice," I said.

"It's traditional," Brian said. "My bubbe did raspberry, but apricot is acceptable."

A tiny little smile flickered at the corner of Pete's mouth. I suspected there had been more than one discussion about Brian's definition of acceptable.

I finished chewing and gave Brian the lawyer look to forestall further rugelach rubrics. "All right, for the purposes of this discussion, you have hired me as your counsel. What's the issue?"

"This is a bit bigger than rugelach, Grace," Pete said.

"How much bigger?"

From their expressions, I suspected I knew what was coming. Brian took a breath. "We saw something at the aquarium."

"Something serious," Pete added, not that he needed to.

"Do you know who you saw?"

Both shrugged.

"Not so sure I could testify," Brian said.

"I was a little closer, and I have a pretty good idea," Pete added, "but my view was partially obscured too."

I lifted the rugelach to my lips, thought better of it. "And you want to know what your responsibility is."

They nodded.

"You have an enforceable legal obligation to tell the truth if and when police ask you what happened," I began. "You may feel a moral obligation to come forward, but in most cases, it would be very difficult to make a legal issue unless there's some extenuating circumstance. As a practical matter, the police would have to want to make an issue of it."

"Do you think they do?" Brian asked.

"In this case?" I asked, looking from him to Pete. "With this—I hesitate to say—victim?"

"Subject?" Pete offered. "So, you're telling us…"

"I strongly suspect the cops will want to leave this one right where it is. An apparently unfortunate mishap with some possible but equivocal evidence of foul play. Literally everyone with any connection to this wants it to go away."

"No one wants to know what happened to Egan?" Brian asked. "Not even his family?"

"As far as I know, there isn't one." I shrugged. Careful not to know too much. "Friend in law enforcement tells me nobody's claimed the body."

"Ouch." Brian shook his head, and Pete winced momentarily. Then both gave grim nods.

"Probably just about right," Pete said.

"Better than a family having to know what he did," added Brian.

"I hope his mother was gone before any of it," I said.

They both looked at me for a long moment.

Then:

"Don't ever change, Grace." Brian patted my arm.

"What?"

"You're thinking like a mother *and* a lawyer. It's a good thing."

"Thanks."

Best thing about friends: They know you.

CHAPTER FORTY-ONE
HAPPY ENDING DANCE

The rugelach were gone, and I was heading back toward Michael and Daniel when the speakers exploded with loud, happy music and the DJ exhorting us to put our hands together for the "Brand-New Mr. and Mrs. Aaaaallllll Kaaaaufman!"

Madge, now in a sparkly and fluffy, but new white dress intended for dancing, and Al— sans yarmulke, prayer shawl, and tie—took the floor for a spin to Sinatra. "Fly Me to the Moon."

Then, the DJ fired up Earth, Wind, and Fire's "September," and their kids rushed out onto the floor, followed by most of the grown-ups, and all the children except for Imani, who was at her table, sulking into a Shirley Temple. Good taste in beverages, anyhow.

Michael hesitated, but I gave him a shove, knowing how much he loves to dance. He shouldn't have to ration his time based on my sore leg. The cut was throbbing a bit from all the standing, and I was starting to get tired.

"Go—enjoy," I pushed him again. "I'm going to go upstairs and check on Nolo."

The kitty was curled up in her carrier by the fireplace. She opened her eyes and accepted an ear scratch, then closed her eyes and went back to sleep. I'd probably wake up with her on my shoulder in the night again, and that was just fine by me.

A quick look at the phone I'd left on the desk gave me one more bit of joy: a message from Lis Allen's parents, saying she'd finished her first week of rehab and was okay so far.

Fingers crossed.

Back downstairs, they'd moved into the constitutionally mandated "Electric Slide," and almost everyone was on the floor, including Michael.

My business if I enjoyed watching him move in full kilt, his face flushed, glowing like he was generating his own spotlight. Yes, he really is the finest man in any room, even if a lot of the other fellas were giving him a run for his money tonight. Of course, he was that much more adorable because he lined up next to Daniel and helped lead him through the steps.

Hot, good partner, good dad…yep, I'm a pretty lucky woman.

The thought made me a little wistful.

"Hey, Gracie!" Old Man Loquat waved me over to the table where he was sitting, a glass of red wine in hand. "Sit by me for a minute. This one's not for me."

"Sure. I'm grounded a little because of the stitches in my leg," I said. "Still, could have been a lot worse."

"Absolutely." He patted my arm, pointed to the floor where Brian and Pete were dancing with Zooey, each taking one of her hands to spin her at every turn. She was giggling, they were beaming, a picture of absolute love and joy. "You know, I'm starting to think we might have another one of these to look forward to."

"I'm thinking the same thing," I agreed. "But let's not push. Let them get there on their own."

"C'mon, Gracie. I'm not going to be here forever. I want to see him happy."

"And you can give him a little time. If you need to jump in and shove, you'll know."

"Maybe so."

Daniel and Cherise had moved to play patty-cake to the beat, as Corinna, Michael, and Clay danced around them. Al and Madge, and the rest of the wedding party, were giving it their best shot too, even Vince. In the far corner, I saw Carla Luciano beckon Moira, who shrugged, and then gamely joined her.

Everybody's getting their happy ending.

So why did I want to cry?

"You're still feeling off balance because of the car crash, aren't you?" the old man asked.

"Little bit." I took a deep breath.

"Close calls will do that." He reached for my hand, his fingers surprisingly warm and strong despite the papery skin. "Look, Gracie, whatever you were afraid of in that water, whatever you thought was going to happen, it didn't happen. You got out and came home to your family."

"I did."

"And it's all that matters. I had more than one scare in the war, and the only way you go forward is to just keep going. It becomes part of you, and everything is sweeter...but it doesn't rule you. Get it?"

"Got it."

"Good." He squeezed my fingers again and let go, smiling.

The DJ switched to a slow song, and Michael turned toward me.

"Now get out there and enjoy a dance with your fella."

"Best idea I've heard all night."

Michael held out his hand, and swirled me in, pulling me close.

He's always attractive, but sometimes, when the light hits him just the right way, he looks downright otherworldly. And just then, a little buzzed from the joy and love, the happy ending we'd all won despite the odds, it felt like a miracle.

So, later, I'd wonder if I imagined what he said.

But I know I didn't.

His lips close to my ear, he whispered: "Next time you're in trouble, Grace, call for the right Archangel."

I pulled back, just enough to look into those glowing green-and-gold eyes.

Michael.

PENUCHE FUDGE

(from a *Farm Journal* recipe)

1 lb. light brown sugar
¾ cup whole milk
⅛ tsp salt
2½ tbsp butter
1 tsp. vanilla

1. Combine brown sugar, milk, and salt in a heavy saucepan.
2. Stir over medium heat until sugar dissolves.
3. Bring to a boil and cook without stirring until it reaches the soft-ball stage (238° on a candy thermometer).
4. Remove from heat, add butter, and cool to lukewarm.
5. Add vanilla and beat until thick and creamy.
6. Pour into a buttered 8x8 pan and cool.

Variation: add another teaspoon of milk at the end, beat until creamy, and use as icing on spice cake, as Grace does when she makes it for Old Man Loquat.

ACKNOWLEDGMENTS

First, thanks, as always, go to my agent, Mira Perrizo at WordLink, and my editors at Turner Publishing, Amanda Chiu Krohn and Ashlyn Inman. Many thanks also to line and copy editors, Aric Dutelle and Lisa Grimenstein.

I'd also like to offer a special word of thanks to Kent Holloway and Britin Haller from Charade Media. Without Kent's willingness to take a chance on Grace, and Britin's sharp editing, the Hit Mom would not have come into the world in her current form.

Finally, to my family of blood, work, and affection, unending gratitude. Thank you for your honesty, your listening, and your support. You pull me through every time.

With love and appreciation,

Nikki Knight

ABOUT THE AUTHOR

Nikki **Knight** is an Author/Anchor/Mom...not in that order. An award-winning weekend anchor at New York City's 1010 WINS Radio, she writes short stories and novels, including the Grace "The Hit Mom" Mysteries and the Vermont Radio Mystery series. Her stories have appeared in *Alfred Hitchcock's Mystery Magazine*, *Mystery Magazine*, *Black Cat Weekly*, online, and in anthologies, and have been short-listed for Derringer and Black Orchid Novella Awards. As Kathleen Marple Kalb, she writes the Ella Shane and Old Stuff mysteries for Level Best Books. She's a Co-VP of the New York/Tri-State Sisters in Crime Chapter and a past VP of the Short Mystery Fiction Society. She, her husband, and their son live in a Connecticut house owned by their cat.